D0200464

To Julia and Mason
—H. C.

Ω

Published by
PEACHTREE PUBLISHING COMPANY INC.
1700 Chattahoochee Avenue
Atlanta, Georgia 30318-2112
www.peachtree-online.com

Text and illustrations © 2021 by Henry Cole

Edited by Kathy Landwehr
Design and composition by Adela Pons

The illustrations were rendered in pencil on paper

Printed in in the United States of America in January 2021 by Lake Book
Manufacturing in Melrose Park, Illinois.
10 9 8 7 6 5 4 3 2 1
First Edition
ISBN 978-1-68263-254-3

Cataloging-in-Publication Data is available from the Library of Congress.

HOMER ON THE CASE

Henry Cole

PEACHTREE
ATLANTA

CHAPTER ONE

At the risk of sounding clichéd, I'll tell you that the fog I was flying through was thick as soup. And not like consommé, more like cream of cauliflower.

I know...you're thinking just how would *I*, a typical homing pigeon, know about things like *soups*?

Because I pay attention, that's how! I read things. Every day, in the newspaper. News! Weather! Advice columns! Recipes!

But I'll explain that later.

Being a homing pigeon means lots of flying. Racing, then finding your way home. I can find my way back home through instinct alone, without any map or compass...just the one in my head.

And flying is serious business, especially in fog: I have to be careful.

I reduced my speed to 35 miles per hour, nearly half my normal racing speed, but even at reduced speeds things can loom suddenly out of dense clouds.

I veered left to miss colliding with the huge Bridgetown water tower. My wing tips were just a caterpillar's length away from the sides of the iron tank. *Close one*, I thought.

With the tower behind me, I looked carefully for a slate-covered spire. In a flash it was there: St. Marco's Church.

A starling gazed at me blankly from his perch on top of the lightning rod as I shot by. "Where's the fire?" he snickered.

I just ignored him and zipped past. When you're racing, seconds count.

I was really breathing heavily now. My pectoralis major was starting to burn. I set my beak to 7 degrees west of north and pitched quickly to the left, and just in time: the needlelike talons of a sharp-shinned hawk swept by, barely missing my chest muscles. I felt a sharp pain at my tail and an invisible push of air as I tumbled in space.

With no time to think, I maneuvered into a series of dives left, right, and down, and landed on a narrow ledge of an apartment building. I was hidden in the fog.

Two tail feathers—my own!—slowly drifted past. The hawk, once again a part of the gray mist, disappeared, disappointed.

"Luck was with me this time," I whispered to myself. All three of my heart chambers were thumping wildly. I took a moment to cautiously look up, then down, left, and right...and then I took off again.

I passed over the tops of some trees, ghostly and vague down below. *Keeler Park*, I thought. *Getting close. But dang it! I'm late!* I knew my time wouldn't be great, thanks to being sidetracked by the hawk.

Soon I saw the familiar red-brown brick of home appear. It was a five-story apartment building. Humans lived inside, but I lived on the top. I could make out my owner Otto down below on the roof. Grandad was standing with him as usual, smiling.

I folded my wings, and with one final thrust I plunged beak-first from the sky, swooping to my landing platform just as the gray-shrouded dawn was turning into a golden, summertime sunrise.

Also as usual, Otto had the gold pocket watch at the ready. I heard him calling even before I landed. "Atta way, Homer! You made it!" He smiled proudly as he clicked a button on the watch. Otto always gave me a hero's welcome, as if I *were* a hero, not just another homing pigeon doing what I do best: coming home.

"How'd he do?" Grandad asked.

"Nineteen minutes! Last time was seventeen. Not your best time, Hom—Homer! Something happened to you! No wonder you're two minutes behind your best time!" He picked me up and held me up to his chin, giving me tiny kisses, as if kisses would help me regrow tail feathers.

This was a little embarrassing, but Otto was prone to overreacting wherever I was concerned. Call it being overprotective. Or get mushy and call it love.

"Looks like Homer might've had a run-in with a hawk," Grandad said. "And looks like it was a close one! But don't worry, Otto. He'll grow new tail feathers in no time."

Otto looked alarmed. "Poor Homer," he said. "Here: I've put down fresh newspaper, a little bit of cracked corn, and your favorite millet mix. Nice clean water. All for you."

I heaved a big sigh and gazed gratefully at my rooftop world. It consisted of a large cage with three sides made of chicken wire and the back covered in wood planks to keep the north wind out. I had a cozy wooden box inside the cage to sleep in, lined with soft, sweet-smelling hay.

The cage had a huge swinging door that was almost

always open. Otto kept it closed with a wooden peg at night, to keep the occasional city raccoon from getting in and stealing my food. But most of the time I was a free-ranging pigeon. I could come and go as I pleased. I think Otto wanted me to have a little freedom, and he trusted me to return to my rooftop. That's one good thing about being a homing pigeon: we always know how to get back home.

I pecked hungrily at the food and gratefully let some of the water trickle down my throat.

Otto grabbed the pencil and clipboard that were kept hanging on a peg. I couldn't help but notice how he always beamed proudly as he carefully recorded my flight times. Even times when I was a minute or two late.

Grandad noticed the cage door wide open. "You know, Otto, you really should keep that cage door closed, 24-7," he said.

Otto gave me another gentle caress. "I know, Grandad. But Homer wouldn't like being cooped up all day. He can come and go as he pleases. He knows where home is."

Grandad gave a little grunt. "Well, he's your pigeon, Otto. Your responsibility. What happens to Homer is on your shoulders. Just remember there are things like hawks out there."

"I know."

The two of them headed down the rooftop ladder. Otto gave me a wink. "See you later, Homer!" he called out.

I felt contented. I had flown well, I had avoided being ripped to shreds by a hawk, and now I had a crop full of cracked corn and millet.

I sighed and stretched my wings, then stepped across the freshly laid-out newspaper. Second only to a morning race, this was the part of the day I enjoyed the most: catching up on world events.

I usually started with the colorful pages. My favorite was a continuing story called *Dick Tracy* about a really smart detective.

Today Tracy was once again trying to foil some crooks. This time, some jewel thieves. The alarm bell over a store went *CLANG!* A voice bubble over Dick's head said *"This is the third jewelry store looted this week! I hope I solve this one before the next store is hit!"*

I cooed contentedly. Dick Tracy was smart. He'd figure it out.

After I looked at the pages with the bright colors I began the serious stuff. I usually went from big headlines to smaller headlines, down each page, story by story. It seemed like the bigger the letters, the more important the story, at least to humans. And sometimes that didn't make sense to me: a story about weapons got big letters, for example, but something about bird populations got tiny letters.

Anyway, I started my morning perusal of the news.

**PRESIDENT
OFFERS NEW
BUDGET PLAN**

Here we go again, I thought. *Yet another new budget plan.*

**DRAMA IN THE MIDDLE
EAST ESCALATES**

"Enough with the drama!" I cooed.

The size of the headlines—and apparently the importance of the news—got smaller and smaller as I walked down and across the pages.

YANKEES SLAM RED SOX 2-1

MISS POWELL WEDS MR. MCGEE

So Miss Powell and Mr. McGee finally got married, I thought absently, glancing at the picture of the newlyweds. *I remember their engagement photo. Gee, they look happy... but then again, they always put happy-looking pictures on this page.*

There were the usual ads for things that humans buy, bargains on ladies' and men's shoes, and sales on lawn chairs and hot dog buns.

NEIGHBORHOOD STREET FAIR

The Marion Street Vendors Association is sponsoring a Street Fair this Saturday. Local shops will offer food and wine tastings, cooking demonstrations, and special discounts. Various artists will be on hand. The band Mangled Scrunchie plays at noon. Fair begins at 9am, rain or shine.

I thought that sounded pretty good. Especially the "food tastings" part. Nice way to spend a Saturday morning. And I bet Carlos would be there.

CHAPTER TWO

So I ended up gliding over to the street fair. Scanning the scene from the air, I saw that Marion Street was blocked off to car traffic, with dozens of booths and tables everywhere. People were jammed shoulder to shoulder as they browsed and sampled. All kinds of smells filled the air...meats and spices, smoky incense, perfumed candles, and bouquets of flowers.

I spotted an empty spot on the sidewalk and fluttered to a landing.

"Hey, Homer!" cooed a familiar voice and, just as I had expected, my friend Carlos ambled up. Carlos was a city pigeon, with striped wings and iridescent neck feathers.

"Hey, Carlos!" I said. "Lots of activity here today, huh?"

"People everywhere. Street fairs are cool."

"Yeah, I love the human-watching."

"I love the way they drop food everywhere!"

We dodged several pairs of human feet, then sat in a protected spot on the curb.

"Thank goodness humans put on things like these fairs," Carlos commented. "What a bounty. Yummy treats everywhere."

"You're always thinking about food."

"Well, you don't have to. You're the lucky one."

"You always say that," I replied.

"But it's true! You don't have to spend most of every day looking for food."

I saw his point, but I thought for a moment. "I work hard for my food," I said. "Racing...timed flights...it can be grueling."

"Yeah, I guess. But think about it: you get food brought to you every day. And what digs! Your house is warm and dry and protected. That's my idea of heaven. I'm lucky if I find a soggy piece of hot dog bun before somebody else does."

I had to agree with Carlos. I had it pretty good. There wasn't a day that I went without fresh food and water. My home *was* warm and dry and protected. Plus, I could come and go whenever I wanted. And with the morning paper, Otto gave me the news of the world every day. Not only could I fly around Bridgetown, I could read about it.

"Speaking of hot dogs," I said, "there's a sale on hot dog buns at the Valu-Mart this week."

Carlos rolled his eyes. "Oh, brother, here we go again."

"And Miss Powell and Mr. McGee got married."

Carlos sighed. "Yeah? Well, what of it? Why do you have to tell me this stupid human stuff? I remember when you told me 'Miss Powell and Mr. McGee Engaged.' Well... what's it to *you*?"

I had to think about that one. I wasn't sure why the human world fascinated me so much. Maybe it was because I lived with humans. Humans took care of me. I raced for them. To see the excitement in their faces when I raced made me excited. It occurred to me that I spent more time in the human world than the bird world.

But I also knew that when I had seen the very first newspaper that had lined my very first cage and I first looked at the pictures in the paper, something inside of me just clicked. I remember I liked Dick Tracy's bright yellow coat. And I could tell what was going on with the expressions on the characters' faces. I began realizing that the little boxes of pictures told a story. It took me a while, but eventually I figured out that all those funny little black scratches on the paper were actually letters of the alphabet.

And I thought: *Hey! There are twenty-six of those different little shapes!* I somehow connected the words and pictures. Then I started putting words together...and then sentences...and then paragraphs.

Then it all started making sense.

There was a big world out there, bigger than a chicken-wire cage.

And I *liked* knowing there was a big world out there. I *liked* knowing where Uruguay was, and I *liked* knowing which ballet was being performed in town, and I *liked* knowing what hints Heloise had.

But sometimes I wanted to *see* Uruguay. And to *see* a ballet. And to thank Heloise, whoever she was, for all her hints.

I glanced at Carlos and sighed. "I...I guess I just think it's interesting," I replied finally. How feeble.

Carlos spotted a bit of Italian sausage that had dropped from a sandwich. "I'll tell you what's interesting," he cooed loudly. "Sausage! And the ants haven't gotten to it yet! Perfecto!"

My crop was still full from breakfast, so I just watched as Carlos pecked at the greasy lump with gusto.

The two of us observed the throngs of people for a while,

avoiding getting kicked or stepped on. A man walked by juggling peaches. A woman tried to calm her crying baby and eat blue cotton candy at the same time.

I watched them all. Humans are fascinating to me.

But then I saw something that really grabbed my attention. A girl was feeding dates to a large green bird perched on her shoulder. My jaw gaped open.

I couldn't remember seeing another bird so closely attached to a human before.

Like me and Otto!

"Look, Carlos," I exclaimed. "There's a bird and a girl!"

Carlos looked bored. "Lucky bird. Being *hand-fed.*"

"But it's sitting on that girl's shoulder!"

"Yeah. So?"

"It's so...unusual! Like they're friends, like Otto and me."

"Mm. Nice."

"The bird is just *sitting* there!"

"I bet that bird is too fat to fly."

I chuckled, thinking about all the bits of food that would drop onto the street and sidewalk during the fair. "I bet you'll be too fat to fly by this afternoon."

Just then there was a loud screech. I glanced over at the green bird.

"*Dates!*" it squawked. "*Dates!*"

I was dumbstruck. "Hey!" I cooed to Carlos. "That bird speaks Human! It just asked the girl for more dates!"

That piqued even Carlos's interest. "Yeah," he murmured.

The girl ambled away through the crowd, the bird bobbing on her shoulder. I gazed after them, mesmerized.

CHAPTER THREE

It rained the morning following the street fair. The city was draped in wet. The idea of racing was out: there was no way Otto would want me to race in that mess. It was a comforting thought to just stay warm and dry in my cozy cage.

Otto was his standard punctual self and came up to the loft to spread the day-old newspaper for my breakfast. I pecked my way across the pages, and, as usual, the bottoms of my pink feet turned black from the newsprint.

I noticed an ad at the bottom of page C3. There was a sale at PetzGalore!

COO-OO-OO-OOL! BIG SALE!

Half Off All Grain-Based Seeds!
Millet, Milo, Corn!
Try Our Buckwheat, Flax, and Oats Mix!

Hmm! I thought. *Not only was going to PetzGalore a great way to spend a rainy day, it was a perfect chance to get some fresh millet and flax...and I was always a pushover for that.* I excitedly pecked and scratched at the ad and flapped my wings to get Otto's attention.

Otto looked at me, slightly perplexed at first. "Hey, Homer! What's wrong with you? You're spreading your food all over the place."

But I kept pecking and flapping and cooing at the ad, then pecked some more.

"You're a goof," Otto said, smiling. He looked at the sky. "Tomorrow should be nice out. Might be a good day for a race."

I sat down on the newspaper, frustrated. Otto hadn't understood me. It had happened before: I had tried to communicate something to Otto, to no avail. No matter how much I flapped and cooed, I couldn't get my message across.

The next morning the weather had cleared. Otto came scrambling up the rooftop stairs way before dawn. He was carrying my smaller travel cage. That could only mean one thing: a race!

Otto slid my cage carefully onto the back seat of Grandad's gray car. I cooed with excitement and paced back and forth, periodically pumping my wings, getting my blood flowing and getting psyched up. I was anxious and ready. I wanted to fly fast for Otto and for Grandad. I noticed Grandad had the gold watch. It would be a timed flight, of course.

He smiled. "Homer will have clean, rain-washed air to fly through. Sky's cleared up. It's a great morning for a flight."

"Where to today, Grandad? Same place as last week? Middleburg?"

"I thought we'd try something a little more challenging for Homer. All the way over to Hillsboro."

Hillsboro! I knew from reading the newspaper that Hillsboro was pretty far. I had seen a picture of the town, with little stone houses tucked into a rolling landscape. It was different from where we lived. I realized I was a little nervous...I hadn't flown that far before.

"Wow," Otto said. "That *is* challenging. But Homer can do it. No problem, right, Homer?" His head popped over the top of the front seat, and in the dim light of the dashboard I saw his grinning admiration.

"No problem!" I cooed.

"You've got quite a pigeon there, Otto," Grandad said. "He's a winner. If you want, we can enter one of the semiprofessional races later this summer."

Otto slapped the headrest enthusiastically. "Heck, yeah! That'd be great!"

"I think he's up to it."

"I know he is. I bet Otto can kick butt. Those professional pigeons had better watch out."

Grandad laughed. "I'll file the paperwork to enter him. We'll have to get in some more serious trials, though."

"Okay!"

The thought of flying in a race with other pigeons got me interested. Early-morning wake-ups, longer and more difficult training flights...I was feeling important!

"Homer reminds me of one of the pigeons I had when I was about your age," Grandad said.

"How so?"

"Well, he's smart...you can tell. There's an intelligence there that's more than what you usually see. And he's got an eagerness. He seems to know exactly what's going on, like he actually knows he's racing, not just getting home fast."

Of course I know I'm racing! What'd they think, I was doing this for exercise? And eager? You bet!

We drove and drove a long way, out into the country. This was definitely going to be my longest flight ever.

As I paced my cage I chuckled to myself, remembering Otto giving me my very first test flight, challenging my homing instinct. It was Otto's first test flight too. Grandad had helped Otto, making sure things went just right.

Those early tests had started out easily enough; the first one had just been a flight across the alley! I was barely beyond being a fledgling back then, with brand-new wing feathers.

But soon the flights were from different parts of the neighborhood, then from all the way across Bridgetown, and then from distant parts of the countryside, on early mornings like this one. And with each flight the process became more and more familiar and I got more and more sure of myself and my instincts.

Off to the east it was gradually shifting from dark to dawn when Grandad pulled the car into an overlook next to the highway. He and Otto set my travel cage on the hood of the car and opened the sliding door.

I checked the position of the rising sun. Instinctively I knew my exact directions. I knew what to do, and I bobbed

my head excitedly left and right to let them know I was
ready to go.

Grandad held the long gold chain and glistening
watch. "Ready when you are, Otto," he said.

"Go, Homer!" Otto shouted.

I took off.

This time there was no morning fog. The air was clear
and smelled of dew and damp pavement and mowed fields.
A pink morning sun peeked between the trees on the
horizon. Long sunrise shadows stretched across the hills.

I zipped toward the city like a feathered bullet.

Down below I saw a car or two winding along the roads,
but I flew in a straight line over the curves and bends. Hills
and dales were all the same to me; my flight path was direct.

After a while I noticed the landscape changing. The
fields, which had been dotted with cows or lined with corn,
were replaced by clusters of houses. I darted over a school
and a shopping center and a wide parking lot speckled with
shiny puddles reflecting the pink sunrise.

Then the buildings began to grow taller and taller,
crisscrossed with busy streets. It wasn't long before I saw
the familiar landmarks of my neighborhood.

In a few minutes I was fluttering to a landing at my loft.

The food dish was empty. I had beaten Otto and Grandad home! Objective achieved!

Soon I heard them climbing the wooden ladder to the rooftop loft.

Otto laughed when he saw me waiting impatiently. "Good boy, Homer!" he shouted.

"A new record," Grandad said, smiling. "Yep, you've got a good racing pigeon there, Otto."

I basked in Grandad's kind words and Otto's loving scratches and strokes.

"Here's your reward, Homer," Otto said. "A fresh batch of your favorite millet mix...*and...*" He held out his palm revealing three wiggling mealworms.

Now that was an unexpected treat! I gobbled them with relish.

Grandad looked at his pocket watch. "Breakfast time for us too. I'll rustle up some blueberry pancakes."

I saw Otto eyeing the antique watch. "Grandad, may I see it again?" he asked.

Otto never seemed to get tired of that gold watch. He practically held his breath as he examined the heavy timepiece, reverently clicking open the cover, and for the millionth time admiring the ivory face and finely etched Roman numerals.

Tucked lovingly inside the cover was the slightly crinkled photograph of a woman, smiling shyly. I watched as a smile curled up the sides of Otto's face. "When you open the watch, you say 'hi' to Grandma, don't you, Grandad?" he asked quietly.

Grandad chuckled. "Yep. That's my favorite picture of her. And I look at my watch every hour. That way I get to see her all day long."

"This photo was taken a long time ago, huh?"

"Yep. Just before the war."

"Grandma sure was pretty."

"The prettiest. Nobody prettier." Grandad pulled back a corner of the black-and-white photo. "Never showed you this before," he said. "See that?"

I arched my neck to see what Grandad was pointing to. Otto traced his finger over fancy letters etched into the gold. I was happy I could read. It said "To Samson with All My Heart from Ada."

Then Otto gently clicked the watch closed. "Thanks, Grandad."

The old man grinned. "Breakfast time for Homer, boy. Get to it."

Finally! I was getting hungry!

Otto spread out fresh newspaper on the cage floor

and scattered mealworms and millet for me. "Here you go, Homer. Yesterday's newspaper. I've already read *Dick Tracy*, the best part. Now my turn for breakfast...blueberry pancakes! See you later, Homer."

I cooed with satisfaction. It was a good morning already. An exhilarating race home, juicy mealworms, yesterday's paper. And the day was just a pup.

I walked slowly across the sheets of newspaper, digesting the world news as well as the mealworms.

EARTHQUAKE SHAKES PERU

DRAMA IN THE MIDDLE EAST CONTINUES

ANCIENT VILLAGE UNEARTHED IN TURKEY

On the comic pages I followed the continuing saga of Dick Tracy. As usual, he was in the middle of solving a crime: a pair of masked crooks were robbing a store. Dick Tracy raced to the scene.

I moved on to the local news page and noticed a small blurb near the bottom.

PARK TO REDEDICATE STATUE

Local authorities will be on hand tomorrow to re-dedicate a statue in Keeler Park. The life-sized bronze soldier was created to commemorate the Battle of Quinoa, in 1917. A fund drive was organized to refurbish and clean the statue.

Keeler Park was nearby, and it was one of my favorite haunts. I knew the statue well; I had landed on it a million times, although recently it had been covered in canvas. Now I understood why.

Hmm, I thought. *Maybe I'll go over there later this morning. Take a look-see.*

But I never thought an ordinary visit to Keeler Park would be the beginning of an adventure.

It was a warm morning, and the park smelled of sycamore trees and lawn clippings. Some early-summer cicadas were starting to thrum. Rows of chairs were set up on the area in front of the statue, and some humans had started to gather there, fanning themselves against the heat. Around the park other humans were walking their dogs or jogging with earphones. Some had taken their places on the green-painted benches that were sprinkled around the park.

An elderly gentleman sat on one of the benches, scattering bread crumbs. A few annoying house sparrows had gathered at his feet, pecking and scratching. The sparrows were always so aggressive and noisy.

But I noticed Carlos was among them, so I settled onto the concrete beside him. "Good morning," I cooed.

"Hey, Homer," Carlos clucked cheerily. "I love this old guy. He's always here with bread crumbs. And the good stuff too. I think this is Pepperidge Farm 12 Grain."

"Excellent!"

The man looked down at me. "Looking for your

breakfast?" he asked. He reached into a plastic bread bag and scattered some more of the crumbs and pieces.

I pecked at the stale crumbs. "They're uncovering the statue this morning, Carlos."

"Ah," he replied. "So that's what all the escandalo is about, eh? They're finally going to take the canvas down so we can land on the statue again?"

"Yep. Big day."

The rows of chairs were filling up as more people moseyed into the park. The pesky sparrows shoved at us, pushing to get at the bread crumbs. As we all pecked at the sidewalk buffet, a lady came up to the bench. I noticed she was carrying a large orange purse. She sat down next to the man with the bread crumbs.

"Testing...testing," boomed a voice from the little stage. The statue dedication ceremony had begun.

A man with a moist forehead and wearing a seersucker suit stood at the microphone. "Good morning, ladies and gentlemen," he said. "Welcome to Keeler Park."

There was a smattering of applause, and the man continued his speech.

Just then I was surprised to see something emerge from the shadow of a trash can. It was a gray rat, dingy and disheveled.

That's odd, I thought. *A rat out and about in the middle of the day. They usually skulk around at night.*

I watched as it silently climbed the ornate iron leg of the bench. The back of the lady loomed above. Her orange purse lay beside her on the bench, drooping open. But the lady was watching the man speaking on the stage, oblivious to the rat.

The rat slunk along the slats of the bench. In a second it was inside the purse.

I gulped, choking a bit on my bread crumbs. *What does he think he's doing?* I said to myself.

A moment later the cautious rat emerged from the bag and traced its steps back along the bench.

My eyes popped out. This time the rat had a glittery gold bracelet around its neck.

Oozing furtively back down the bench leg, the rat darted across the pavement, between trash cans and flower beds, then paused in front of a storm drain.

"Hey!" I cooed loudly. "Drop that! Hey!"

But no one paid me any attention. Carlos and the others were busy pecking at breadcrumbs. I flapped and cooed loudly, to no avail. The rat disappeared into the drain.

I flew over to the front of the bench and fluttered in

front of the woman's ankles. "Lady!" I cooed again, as emphatically as I could. "Look over there! That dirty rat stole your bracelet! He's getting away!"

But the woman gave a little scream and waved her hands at me. "Shoo! Shoo! Nasty pigeon!" she exclaimed. "Go away!" She grabbed her purse and swung it at the whole group of us. Carlos and the throng of sparrows took off in a flurry of wings, and the woman trotted down the sidewalk shrieking, still swinging her purse and waving hysterically.

"But...but...*lady!*" I insisted, but the woman had disappeared among the people.

I heard the bread crumb gentleman giggle. "Now *that* lady is messed up!" he said. "I wonder who pulled her chain?"

I gazed after her, frustrated. And puzzled.

CHAPTER FOUR

I pretty much forgot about the incident in the park until a few days later. It was a typical day, and I woke up as usual to the sound of Otto tromping up the rooftop steps, spreading out the clean newspaper and sprinkling millet on it. Also as usual we had some one-on-one time consisting of me getting lots of gentle chin scratching and feather stroking.

Then it was breakfast time for him and for me. After absentmindedly pecking at my millet I turned my attention to the daily news.

I examined the front page, and halfway down I found exactly what I knew would be there.

THEFT IN KEELER PARK WORRIES NEIGHBORHOOD

Mrs. Marjorie Brittlebank was robbed during Saturday's Quinoa Statue festivities at Keeler Park. An expensive gold bracelet was stolen from the wealthy socialite's bag as she observed the statue unveiling ceremony. No suspects have been identified. The theft remains a mystery.

Hmph, I thought. *This is no mystery! I know exactly who took the bracelet. That ratty-looking rat!*

I pondered the theft while slowly padding across the paper to the comics. There again was my favorite, Dick Tracy, who was talking into his two-way wrist radio. A voice bubble had him saying *"I'm on the trail of the crooks!"*

In the second panel of the comic, Tracy was hiding near a jewelry store, cloaked in the shadows. *"Now to keep surveillance on the joint,"* he said.

The third panel showed him watching over the store as the moon rose over the city.

I put some thoughts together in my head.

Hmm...Surveillance. That must mean keeping an eye on things and looking for clues. Maybe I need to go do some "surveillance" at Keeler Park.

I flew back to the park to investigate. The small stage near the statue had been removed, and several pigeons were gleaning what remained of yesterday's potato chips and sandwich crumbs. Carlos was there having his breakfast. I settled onto the sidewalk beside him.

"Hey, Carlos. Remember the lady that screamed at me the other day? The lady with the orange pocketbook?"

Carlos looked up from his crumbs. "Yeah sure, I

remember," he cooed. "Screaming like she had eaten a hot samosa!"

"Well, I know something about her. Right before she started swinging her purse around? And acting crazy? Her bracelet was stolen...that very day, on that very bench. I saw it happen!"

Carlos looked doubtful. "What do you know about any bracelet?" he asked.

"I saw the bracelet stolen, then I read about it in the newspaper. Front-page headline. She's a rich lady, and she carried some of her jewels around with her. Her bracelet was stolen right from under her nose...and I saw who did it."

"Who?"

"A rat. A very disreputable-looking rat. It climbed in her purse, grabbed the bracelet, and then took off."

Carlos looked skeptical. "But why would a rat do that? What's a rat want with a fancy bracelet? You can't eat it."

"I don't know, but I wish I did."

"Why? What's it to you?"

"I witnessed the whole thing!"

"So?"

I thought for a second. There was just something *not*

right about the whole thing. The rat was so devious. And to have a newspaper item printed about it...that must mean it's important. And I knew about it. I had to act somehow.

"That bracelet is valuable for some reason," I replied. "You're right, you can't eat it. But a sneaky rat stole it, and the old lady wants it back. That's all."

Carlos shrugged. "Rats are loco. Humans are loco. Period."

"Some humans are, but not all. Not Otto and Grandad. They're...well, they're my family."

That comment got a stare from Carlos. "Family, eh? Well, they keep you fed, I gotta admit that."

"Just do me a favor. Would you keep your eyes open for any rats snooping around?

Carlos shrugged and continued with his breakfast. "Okay. You got it."

I took off to the other end of the park to expand my surveillance area. I found a quiet part of the walkway under a bench and sat, watching the morning crowd.

A man had taken off his jacket and was writing something on his newspaper. On another bench, a woman was immersed in a book. An older man was snoozing nearby. Someone was pushing a baby stroller, humming a tune.

I studied the trash cans and the storm drains. There were no shadowy rats anywhere. Things were getting, well...dull.

But then over near some azaleas I spotted two cats: an orange one and a gray-and-white one. Neither wore collars. Their fur was matted and dingy. One was missing the last two inches of its tail.

No one else seemed to notice them sauntering silently from bush to bush. But something looked oddly suspicious about them to me, and I watched them closely.

The two cats stopped at the edge of the sidewalk and lurked for a moment behind a water fountain. The orange cat strolled out into the crowd and lay down on the sidewalk. Suddenly it began meowing piteously, yowling and howling like its paw was caught under a rocking chair.

Everyone looked up.

"Oh! The poor kitty!" one woman cried out.

The man put down his newspaper and quickly trotted over to the cat, who continued to writhe and moan on the sidewalk. He bent over. "Hello, kitty. You okay?"

Several others gathered around. "Look, he's missing part of his tail!" someone said. "Should we call a vet?"

The humans were so distracted by the yowling orange

cat, they didn't notice the gray-and-white one. It darted over to the bench where the man had been sitting, and in half a second it had hopped up on the bench. It poked its head into the man's suit jacket pocket. A moment later it scooted away...with a gold ink pen in its mouth!

Well! Another robbery! And I saw the whole thing—again!

"Hey!" I clucked loudly. "Stop! Thief!" I took to the air to follow him just as the orange cat bounded up off the sidewalk and took off like a streak into the bushes.

"What was that all about?" I heard one of the humans say.

"Crazy cat!" said another.

The gray cat raced through the bushes and the shadows, the gold pen flashing as it passed through patches of sunlight.

"Stop! Stop, I say!" I cooed again and again, giving chase.

The cat came to the edge of the sidewalk where the street began and paused at a storm drain. I saw him look up at me. His eyes were green-gold, large, and panicky. A second later he and the gold pen had disappeared into the dark of the drain.

I flew back to the water fountain. The man who had lost his gold pen was on his hands and knees, searching for it under the bench and along the sidewalk. He was clearly worried.

"I just had it," he said to anyone nearby. "I know I did." He stood up, patted himself down, and scratched his head. "I was working on the crossword puzzle...*in ink!*...and that cat started meowing, and I got up to check on it...and now the pen is gone!"

"Did you check your jacket?" a lady asked.

The man looked at her and frowned. "Of course I checked my jacket. It was a very valuable Le Pompeuse pen!"

I guess he wasn't kidding about its being valuable, because soon I noticed that a police officer was on the scene.

I was perplexed. Here was another blatant, middle-of-the-day theft in the park. And I seemed to be the only witness. "Those two cats and that mangy-looking rat have to be in cahoots," I clucked.

I had to figure out how...and *why?*

CHAPTER FIVE

Two days later, as was my usual morning routine, I pecked at the cracked corn and millet sprinkled over the previous day's newspaper and searched the headlines. Sure enough, there it was, this time in even larger type.

ANOTHER THEFT VEXES RESIDENTS

I cocked my head and thought. A rat swipes a gold bracelet. A cat steals an expensive pen. It couldn't be a coincidence; there had to be a connection. But a rat and a couple of cats? What could possibly bring them together?

I decided I needed more clues.

That meant more surveillance.

This time I posted myself at the storm drain near the park and waited for the thieves to show themselves again. Positioning myself on the sidewalk between the flattened dark wads of discarded chewing gum, I studied the storm drain, carefully dodging human feet as they passed back and forth. I made a mental note of everyone that passed by while still keeping an eye on the drain. But nothing poked its nose out of the drain, nothing darted down into it, and no one suspicious passed by.

I heard a familiar cooing and a flurry of wing feathers as Carlos settled next to me.

"Good morning, Homer! How's it going? Caught any bracelet thieves?"

"Morning, Carlos. Nope, haven't caught the thieves, but things are getting even more interesting. There are two cats involved now."

"Say what?"

"Two cats made off with a gold pen yesterday."

Carlos looked blasé. "Hmph. Why would a cat want a pen?"

Just then we heard a shrill bark. "Hey! Out of the way!" yapped a snappy voice.

Carlos and I shuffled aside as a pair of puffy poodles marched past, each on one end of a bright red leash. At the other end of the leashes was a thin, elegant lady.

The poodles stopped and sniffed around. One of them had a collar of black leather dotted with a ring of shiny green stones that sparkled and twinkled. The other's collar was identical, but with pink stones. They glared at Carlos and me.

"What are *you* staring at?" one of them snipped.

"Huh? M-me?" I stuttered.

"Yes, you. You're staring." She turned to the other poodle. "Such bad manners! Olivia, the streets are just *full* of riffraff these days."

"You said it, Miss Pitty-Pat," Olivia agreed. "Let's move along."

The two poodles led their owner down the street and disappeared into the crowd.

"Hmph," I said, watching the poodles sashay away. "And *I'm* the one with the bad manners!"

"No kidding," Carlos agreed. "Guess they woke up on the wrong side of the doggie bed. Well, I gotta go. See you later, Homer."

"See you later, Carlos. Will you keep me posted if you see anything unusual?"

"Sure will, Homer!"

The morning turned into afternoon. Nothing out of the ordinary had happened, although at one point I did spot the girl with the green bird across the street. I watched them intently; the bird was focused on preening as it perched on the girl's shoulder, while the girl window-shopped. They slowly idled down the sidewalk and disappeared around the corner.

I was curious: was the green bird a racing bird?

I decided to call it a day and headed home.

The next morning at breakfast during my walk across the newspaper I saw that square-jawed Dick Tracy was still on the trail of the jewel thieves. His stakeout of a fancy store had seemed pointless. *"Night after night, watching. Ninety percent of a detective's job is waiting and watching. Boring stuff..."* said Tracy's voice bubble. *"But I have to keep at it. Have to break this case!"*

Apparently keeping up surveillance when there wasn't any breakthrough was tedious stuff. But on a hunch I decided to take up my post at the storm drain again. The morning felt nearly the same as the one before; I noticed many of the same humans doing similar things on their daily routines. Nothing remarkable happened.

I was getting discouraged.

Just then I heard the jingle of dog tags and the little clippy sound of claws on sidewalk, and I glanced up the street. There they were on their morning stroll again, prissy Olivia and Miss Pitty-Pat, with their upturned noses and smug faces. The elegant lady holding their leashes was laden with fancy shopping bags. They passed by me and then stopped outside Le Bon Vivant pastry shop. The poodles waited, looking bored and totally ignoring the rest of the world as the lady tied their leashes to a parking meter and then went inside the shop.

I went back to my storm drain surveillance. The daylong watch was going slowly. I hadn't spotted anything out of the ordinary, and the steady drone of passing feet and street noise made me sleepy. I was about to doze off. But suddenly I jerked wide awake as the two poodles began furiously barking and yipping, sounding like firecrackers going off.

"Help!" Miss Pitty-Pat shrieked. "Help!"

"Thief!" yelped Olivia.

Their startled owner had emerged from the pastry shop, dropping her shopping bags beside her on the sidewalk. She looked stricken as she untied the leashes from the parking meter.

I couldn't believe it as I watched two gray rats leap from within one of the bags and each emerge with a jewel-encrusted dog collar. The bag tipped over and some brightly colored tissue paper floated across the sidewalk. The poodles barked in terror, but the rats bared their teeth threateningly before tearing off down the street, each with a fancy collar looped around its neck.

It was over in a moment. Before I had time to blink the rats had darted through holes of a wobbly manhole cover and disappeared.

For just a second the woman was stunned, too, but then she shouted hysterically. "My darlings! What's wrong? Police! Police!" She picked up the empty PetzGalore shopping bag and held it upside down. "My new collars! Police!"

Another robbery, again in broad daylight.

The distraught woman talked with a police officer, who took notes in a little pad. Soon a small crowd had gathered around her. Another woman showed up and began taking pictures. The poodle sisters were frantic, jumping and yelping.

"They came out of nowhere!" Olivia shrieked. "Our collars! They took our brand-new collars! We had just picked them out at PetzGalore!"

"They were priceless!" added Miss Pitty-Pat, stretching out her neck and yipping wildly. "Real synthetic emeralds! Real synthetic amethysts!"

As irritating as they had been, I did feel sorry for the two poodles. I flapped over to them.

"Had you seen them before, the two rats?" I asked.

Olivia looked at me. I could see in her eyes that she was truly scared. "All of a sudden, there they were. They were horrible! We were defenseless!"

"But had you seen them before?"

"Never!"

Miss Pitty-Pat was trembling with distress. "Those... those hairy *beasts!*"

I tried to comfort the two dogs. "I saw where they went. I'll find your collars." I said it, but I wasn't sure how I was going to accomplish it.

The crowd began to disperse. The police officer had taken his notes, but he had little to go on. There was no one to arrest.

With not a little effort the elegant lady lifted a poodle under each arm and shakily staggered down the street.

I was beginning to feel that there was only one way to find the culprits, and that was to go underground. I suspected that the storm drains would somehow lead me to the band of thieves.

Afternoon shadows were stretched out in long patterns across the street and sidewalk. If I was going investigate underground, it was too late in the day to start. I headed home.

Two days of surveillance had turned up...nothing. The newspaper reported...nothing. Then on the third day I finally got some news.

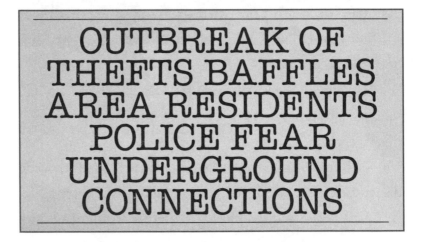

OUTBREAK OF THEFTS BAFFLES AREA RESIDENTS POLICE FEAR UNDERGROUND CONNECTIONS

Underneath the headline was a photo of the elegant lady, looking emotionally overwrought, with her two fancy poodles.

I spent all morning and afternoon pondering the events of the last few days: the lady with the orange purse, the mangy cats, the yelping poodles, the stolen treasures.

It was getting dark. The distant streetlamps cast a dim, silvery light across the latest newspaper that lay beneath my feet.

I scanned the front page yet again. The two poodles stared up at me. I remembered them barking in a panic and the awful way the rats bared their teeth.

And then my feathers ruffled in excitement. I had an idea.

What if I could get Otto to understand that I knew something about the thefts?

A moment later I was pecking and scratching at the newspaper article, tearing it out as carefully as I could. I pulled and yanked and ripped until I had most of it, although Miss Pitty-Pat's head in the photograph was torn in two.

Then I flew to Otto's windowsill.

I knew exactly which window was Otto's; there was a

model plane hanging from the curtain rod. The light was on, and I could see Otto lying on his bed, reading a *Dick Tracy* comic book.

I was so excited to show Otto the clipping, I nearly crash-landed into the window! I fluttered and waved the newspaper photo, pacing back and forth across the sill.

Otto looked up, annoyed at the interruption. But then he saw that it was me, trying boldly to get his attention and brandishing the piece of newspaper. "What the...?" he said.

I cooed loudly as Otto lifted the window sash and the scrap of newspaper drifted to the floor.

"Homer! What are you doing here?" Otto asked. I watched as he picked up the clipping, studying it closely. "And what's this all about?" He looked at me blankly. "Homer, I think you're losin' it. Why are you bringing shredded newspaper into my room?"

Then his eyebrows arched in surprise. "Homer! Are you starting to build a nest?"

Oh, brother!

"No!" I cooed in frustrated protest. I paced back and forth across the windowsill, cooing and clucking but of course making no sense to Otto.

Otto gently picked me up. "Come on," he said, stroking my neck feathers. "Let's get you back up on the roof. You'll have to make your nest up there. Grandad may not like it if he sees you in my room. You've got a great big cage, made just for you."

He carried me through the apartment and carefully tucked me back into my cage.

I sighed. What had I expected Otto to do? Figure out what I was trying to tell him? Waving a picture from the newspaper at him wasn't going to help. It had been a crazy idea.

I'd have to come up with plan B.

I glanced at the funny papers. Dick Tracy was still monitoring activity at the jewelry store, hunched and hidden in the shadows. A voice bubble showed Tracy talking to himself. *"Perseverance,"* he was saying. *"Stick with it. That's the key. The crook always comes back to the scene of the crime."*

Perseverance, I thought. *Stick with it.*

Of course! Dick Tracy was right. I wouldn't be able to help solve these thefts unless I was persistent.

I resolved to be like Dick Tracy, the great comic strip detective, and keep at it.

6

CHAPTER SIX

The next day was warm and breezy. I flew to the park, looking for Carlos. I was itching to find out if he had seen any unusual activity. But although I scanned the usual places, I didn't see Carlos's familiar stripes anywhere.

I circled the area around the trickling fountain, flew around the statue, and finally landed on the back of one of the green benches.

And then I cooed with excitement. Across a bit of mowed lawn I spotted the girl and her green bird from the street fair! The girl sat on a bench, chatting away to the bird. She held a plastic sandwich bag of grapes and Brazil nuts. The bird was perched on her shoulder, as I'd seen it before.

"You've got a good appetite today," the girl said. "One more grape, Lulu."

So...the green bird's name was Lulu.

Lulu grabbed the grape and then glanced over at me. "Hello!" she squawked.

"Hi there," I cooed.

I shuffled closer, balancing across the back of the bench and admiring her lime-green feathers, which were dotted with scarlet around her large yellow eyes. She was certainly nothing like any other bird I had seen. She was exotic! In fact, I was a little reticent to speak to her.

"I—I've seen you around before," I ventured. "At the street fair. You're not from around here, are you? Are you visiting? Or a new resident?"

"*Brand*-new," the parrot replied. "Just arrived. Name's Lulu."

"Homer," I responded. I bobbed my head and bowed. "Nice to meet you, Lulu. Have you been to the park before?"

"Once or twice. Looks like this is the place to be, if the weather's nice...and if Charlotte here feels like it."

"I've never seen such colorful feathers."

"Thank you."

"Warm day today," I said.

"I love it," Lulu replied, sighing happily and fluffing her feathers. "My favorite thing is warm sunshine. Also, Brazil nuts."

I glanced at the young girl, who absently offered me a tidbit of a nut. She smiled.

"Thank you," I cooed, and then pecked quickly and lightly at her hand. The nut was delicious. I gestured at the girl. "Is that Charlotte?" I asked.

Lulu nodded. "She is very nice. I can understand a lot of what *she* says, but she can't understand *me* unless I speak Human. She's teaching me."

"Teaching you what?"

"To speak Human."

"Really? Wow!"

"Just watch."

Lulu stretched out her neck and squawked. "*Grape!*"

Charlotte grinned and reached into the bag, presenting Lulu with the plump purple fruit.

"Nice!" I cooed. "You have her well trained!"

Lulu squawked again. "*Grape!*"

Another grape appeared from the sandwich bag.

"Nice!" I cooed again. I couldn't believe it. "I could never make those sounds, Lulu! You're amazing."

"Thanks," Lulu replied. "I've gotten pretty good at Human sounds. Charlotte and I chat all the time." But then she deflated a bit. "There's the one bad thing, though," she said, holding up her left wing. "Clipped. Can only fly short distances. The thought of you, circling high over the trees, makes me very jealous."

"Ooh. Sorry."

"Oh, thanks, but I'm used to it."

"Does it hurt?"

"Nope. Charlotte takes me to the vet every so often and my flight feathers are cut."

"Why?"

"It keeps me from flying away...as if I'd have some idea of where to fly to!"

"But...what about if you ran across a hawk? That happened to me recently. My wing feathers proved invaluable!"

"What's a hawk?"

"A bird that thinks you and I would make great meals, that's what! There could be one swooping out of the sky any minute."

Lulu glanced at the sky. "Oh. Well, I don't know. I've never been one to be outside much. At first I lived with other birds like me. It was so long ago and I was so little, I can't remember much of it...but there were lizards...and fish tanks...and noisy kids poking around. That's where my wings were clipped the first time. Charlotte brought me home one day and I've been with her ever since. She's trained me with words, lots of Human words. Recently she's brought me here, to the park, and we take walks around the city, but most of the time I'm in my cage at home. I don't get around like you seem to."

"Yeah, I'm lucky I guess. I can come and go as I please, and I never lose track of home. I'm a homing pigeon."

Lulu looked at me questioningly. "Hmm?"

"A homing pigeon. I can find my way home from anywhere. I never get lost."

"That must be a comforting thought."

"I've been in training. I'll be racing with other homing pigeons later this summer."

"Homer, I'm jealous!" She lifted her clipped wing. "Well, I may be missing some feathers, but there are worse things, I guess. At least I can sit in the sun, watch the day go by, full of grapes and Brazi—"

Lulu was interrupted by a flutter of wings and iridescent neck feathers as Carlos landed next to the bench. "Homer! Homer!" he clucked, pacing quickly back and forth. "You gotta come quick! Something has happened!"

"What's up, Carlos?" I asked.

"Another theft! This time I saw it!"

Lulu ruffled her feathers in excitement. "Saw what? What happened? Where?"

Carlos suddenly took notice of Lulu. "Uh...who's your friend?" he asked me.

"Carlos, this is Lulu. Lulu, this is Carlos."

"Pleasure," Carlos said.

"The pleasure's mine, Carlos," Lulu replied. "What's all this about a theft?"

"Lulu, I've witnessed several recent thefts," I said earnestly. "Very unsavory thieves stealing right from under the noses of totally unsuspecting victims. Right here in this park."

"No kidding?"

"Totally true."

Carlos flapped his wings. "And now something else... another one...has happened. Homer, you gotta come quick, I'm tellin' ya!"

"Okay, Carlos." Suddenly I felt both brave and important, a strange combination for me. I gave Lulu a little bow. "I have to go. It was nice meeting you, Lulu. I'll look for you again here in the park."

"Nice meeting you too, Homer. And you, Carlos. Good luck!"

With that, I flew off across the trimmed park lawn with Carlos leading the way.

Carlos shouted over his shoulder. "I was keeping a lookout, just like you said I should. I was at the north end of the park. Then outta nowhere this old geezer starts jumping up and down, shouting about his watch. 'Where's my watch? Where's my watch?' he shouts over and over, like a maniac. I figured it was another theft, and I went looking for you."

"Thanks. Good surveillance."

We made a slight circle in the air before dropping to the ground near one of the green benches. A small group of people had clustered around an elderly gentleman, and a police officer had arrived. I squirmed and dodged in between the feet of the people standing around, and then I looked up.

"...and it was given to *me* by *my* father," the old man was saying . "It was solid gold. And...it was very sentimental to me. It had a photo inside, a photo of my deceased...my Ada. And it's gone!" The old man's voice choked.

I gulped. I recognized the voice.

"That's *Grandad!*" I said to Carlos.

CHAPTER SEVEN

Now I was really perplexed, even a little angry. The thefts in Keeler Park had become...*personal*. I was sure that I knew who had taken Grandad's watch, certain that those same dirty rats and dingy cats were responsible, and I was determined to expose them as the crooks.

My problem was figuring out how to get Otto to understand.

I raced home like I was on fire. I don't know if I had ever flown so fast. I made it back in under a minute.

And as luck would have it, Otto was on the rooftop, putting fresh hay in my roosting box. I skidded to a halt in front of him and immediately began performing what I thought was a pretty good reenactment of each of the thefts I had seen. I fluttered and swooped and cooed and used every means I knew to get the idea across.

The idea didn't get across.

Otto stared at me, mouth agape. "Homer...you okay?"

he stammered. "You're acting a little...a little nutsy-coo-coo."

I had never felt so exasperated. If only I could make sense to Otto!

Just then we heard feet slowly plodding up the stairs, and Grandad appeared. He looked droopy, gray, and lost. He stared at us, looking so very sad.

"Grandad...what's wrong?" Otto said.

"My watch. It's...gone. Stolen!"

He was almost in tears. Otto went over to him and hugged him around the waist. "What happened?"

"I don't know! I was in the park. I had the watch...and then I didn't."

"I'll go to the park right now and hunt for it!"

"We looked everywhere, Otto. There's no point in going back there. The police came, and other kind folks helped me search. We looked under every bench and behind every bush, but it's nowhere to be found." He turned and made his way back down the stairs, clearly heavyhearted.

I looked at Otto. His mind was clicking, I could tell. He wanted to find that watch.

And I wanted to help.

The next day Otto came up to the roof with the morning paper. There was a headline about the thefts in big letters on the front page. Otto read the article aloud, looking very perturbed. The article wasn't much help; the police were stumped. Since so many people had reported items missing after spending time in the park, news of another theft was now becoming commonplace.

PETTY THEFTS RAMPANT AT KEELER PARK

The crime rate at Keeler Park has escalated to an unprecedented high this week as petty thefts in the park continue. Mayor Tomlinson has expressed her concern and offered a reward to anyone with information about the thefts. No suspects have been found, and police report no leads.

The article went on to suggest that anyone using the park should be on the alert and should keep his or her valuables closely guarded.

Otto absently cleaned my cage, lining it with pages of newspaper and looking a little distant. I could tell he was thinking of the watch. After a few gentle strokes to my chin, he went down the stairs.

I walked across the newspaper pages, thinking. This was new, this feeling of uneasy frustration. I paced back and forth, head bobbing, deep concentration, pondering. I felt a little helpless. I didn't know what to do next, outside of more scouting around.

Finally I turned to scan the comics. What would Dick Tracy do? There he was in his yellow coat, this time surreptitiously observing two suspicious-looking characters near a jewelry store. A few panels later he was watching them again, this time outside another jewelry store in a different part of town. He was watching. Keeping track. Making mental notes.

"Hmm," I cooed.

I flew to Keeler Park for more surveillance. On the way I found Carlos near one of the food cart vendors.

"Nice going yesterday, Carlos," I said, landing beside him. "Thank you."

"No problem. How's Grandad doing?"

"It's bad. He looks like someone let the air out of him."

"I'm sorry, Homer. I know you're always saying he's a nice old guy."

"Yes, he is. The theft of his watch has him really down. And according to the newspaper, they still have no idea who the crooks are. I can't figure out a way to tell any humans who they are. And I haven't seen hide nor hair of the culprits. You didn't see anybody steal the gold watch, did you?"

"Nah. They'd taken off by the time I saw what was happening. But I did see your friend Lulu over in the park this morning, near the statue."

"Thanks, Carlos."

I flew to the statue area of the park and was happy to see Lulu and Charlotte underneath the huge sycamore. I landed with a flourish beside their bench.

"Good morning, Lulu!" I clucked. "News to report."

"Morning, Homer. What's the latest? Was it an actual theft yesterday?"

"Yep, not only was there a theft, but the gold watch that was stolen was a prized possession of my owner's."

"No kidding?"

"No kidding. A solid gold watch."

"Wow. I wonder who the thief could be."

"You want to help me find out?"

"Well, yeah, but how could I help?"

"Be observant. Look for any suspicious behavior. Anything...odd. Anything out of the ordinary. Especially be on the lookout for unsavory cats and rats."

"But what do I *do*, Homer? I mean, what if I see something and you aren't nearby? Remember, I can't fly. Not very far anyway."

That made me pause.

"Good question," I said. "How about this: if you see something, say something. Tell Charlotte. Try to make her understand. But for now, just keep your eyes open, monitor the park, and look for details."

Lulu's eyes widened and she clacked her mandibles. "That I can do. You can count on me."

I bowed my head up and down excitedly. "I'm going to watch things from the other side of the park. That way we'll cover more territory. Thanks, Lulu."

That night I couldn't sleep. I was restless and troubled and my mind was full of thoughts. I paced the cage awhile.

Then I glided down to the kitchen window.

A cheery glow came from inside, but the scene at the kitchen table was anything but cheery. Otto sat with Grandad, who was still clearly upset and was despondently twisting the gold watch chain over and over between his fingers. It was all that was left of his antique timepiece.

"I was just sitting on the bench, enjoying the day," Grandad was saying. "I looked down to check the time... and it was just the chain! I know the watch had been there, just like any other day. I know I had it, because I had just held it in my hand! I remember I checked the time! 8:52!" His expression drooped. "At least...I think I did."

This all sounded too familiar. I would have bet anything that the shiny gold watch had caught the eye of either a seedy-looking rat or a pair of shabby tabbies.

I studied the sad pair sitting at the kitchen table. Otto seemed nearly as distressed as his grandad. "Are you sure you didn't drop it?" he asked. "Was it on the chain securely?"

Grandad frowned. "I know it was *there*. One minute I was checking the time, and the next minute the watch was gone. It just...vaporized! It's like it walked off by itself!"

I watched the scene, distraught and vexed. I didn't know how I was going to do it, but I was going to find out how to get Grandad's watch back.

8

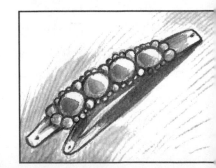

CHAPTER EIGHT

As promised, early the next morning Grandad and Otto had planned another test flight for me, to prepare for the late-summer race. This time I was taken out even farther and in a different direction. The three of us rode in the darkness and in silence, as though we were making a test flight because we had to, not because we wanted to. There was just something missing without the gold watch there.

I zipped along and made it back in great time—no fog, no hawks—but when I arrived back at the rooftop, Otto and Grandad were less than enthusiastic.

They had a new plastic watch with a timing function to replace the stolen one. It was nothing like the grand and glistening gold watch. Even hearing my flight time reported off this watch wasn't as exciting. Grandad looked sad and deflated, and both he and Otto were quiet and hardly spoke to one another.

Otto gave me some gentle caresses and nuzzled me

against his chin. Grandad looked at us. "Your grandma missed this test flight, Otto," he said. I knew that he meant that without her photo watching over us, the test flight just wasn't the same.

Later that day, I think in an effort to make the best of things, Otto did something he did only on special occasions: he took me out shopping with him. He had finally noticed another ad for a sale on bird supplies at PetzGalore, and without my attempts at helping. Plus, Otto liked the way that Mr. Petz made a special mix of wheat, oats, millet, flax, cracked corn, and thistle...just for me.

"Ah! Otto! And you brought Homer!" Mr. Petz announced as the door jingled and Otto and I entered the store, with me balanced on the top of Otto's cap. "My best customers! Welcome to PetzGalore." He petted the top of my head with his plump fingers. "And have I got something for you two. Already bagged, the best in the shop: Homer's Special Mix. I know you like Homer to eat the best, always. Wheat, oats, red millet, flax, cracked corn...and I added some peanut pieces. Homer, you're gonna love it!"

I cooed at the sight of the brown bag of seed. It was nice to hear Otto sounding cheerful again, as he slid his money across the counter. "Thanks, Mr. Petz. That's terrific. Say hello to Mrs. Petz for me. And Grandad says to tell you hello too."

"Ah, yes, and all the best to him. How's he doing?"

"Um...fine."

"Your 'fine' doesn't sound so fine! What's the matter, Otto?"

"Well, I guess Grandad isn't so fine. His gold watch was stolen. We think it may have been one of the Keeler Park thefts."

"No kidding? Oh, that's too bad. Your Grandad loved that watch, this I know for sure. And I've been reading about those thefts...the world just isn't safe anymore."

"Yes, sir. Well, we've gotta go now, Mr. Petz. Bye. Thank you!"

I cooed "thank you" too.

"Bye, Otto. Bye, Homer. Be careful! Tell your Grandad how sorry I am."

We made our way home by going down Donovan Street and then through Keeler Park, taking the diagonal path that cut the park in half. It was wonderful taking a walking trip, and I bobbed along on Otto's cap, savoring the air beneath the large elms and sycamores that lined the sidewalks. I could see things up close, things I would have missed by flying over them. The tall trees kept the sidewalks cool and muffled the noises of the city.

Otto came to an abrupt halt beneath a large sycamore and I almost toppled off his cap. He had spotted Charlotte, with Lulu perched on her shoulder, sitting on one of the green park benches. Charlotte was stroking Lulu's green wing feathers.

Lulu had seen us approaching. "Hey, Homer!" she squawked.

"Hello, Lulu!" I cooed back.

We watched to see what Otto and Charlotte would do next.

Otto walked up to the bench and then just stared at Lulu. I could see he was in awe. Lulu was gorgeous. And Charlotte was cute too.

"Nice bird," he remarked at last, a little shyly.

"Thanks," Charlotte replied.

"Can I pet him?" Otto asked.

"She's a 'she,' and yes, you can. But gently."

"Yeah, I know," Otto said. "I'm gentle. I have a bird too. This is Homer." He pointed up.

"Well, you know you never can tell," Charlotte

commented. She smiled at me on top of Otto's cap. Obviously she didn't recognize me from the other day in the park. "Some people get all grabby. Some people think they know everything, and then they do the absolute wrong thing."

"That's true," Otto said.

"Homer looks nice. He's funny. He keeps looking down at me and Lu—oh, this is Lulu."

Otto finally reached up, cradled me in the crook of his arm, and brought me down to conversation level.

"Yeah, Homer's a good bird. My name's Otto."

"I'm Charlotte. So do you want to pet Lulu? She's super used to people. Never nips. Never bites."

Otto reached out and stroked Lulu along the nape of her neck. "She's really pretty," he said. He noticed Lulu was sitting on a small towel draped across Charlotte's shoulder. "What's with the towel?"

"Claws. Lulu's are sharp. The towel keeps her from gripping into my skin as she rides along. She has perfect balance, since she's so used to sitting on my shoulder when we go out. Also...it's a poop guard. You never know..."

Otto nodded. "Got it."

Lulu looked embarrassed, and she glanced at the sky for a moment.

Charlotte continued. "She's an Amazon. Amazon parrot. I've had you ever since you were a teensy little chick, haven't I, Lulu?" She nuzzled Lulu against her cheek.

"Since she's a parrot, she talks, right? Lulu wanna cracker?"

Charlotte chortled. "Oh, Lulu knows lots of words. It takes lots and lots of training. I've been teaching her since I got her. I think now she knows maybe a hundred words for things."

"That's so cool."

Charlotte dug into a sandwich baggie and pulled out a slice of green pepper. "Lulu, what's this?"

It was time for Lulu to show off.

"*Pepper!*" Lulu squawked.

Otto grinned. "Wow. Do another one!"

"Lulu, what's this?" This time Charlotte took a fancy clip from her hair and held it up.

Lulu glanced at me. "Here we go," she sighed. "*Hair clip!*"

"Wow!" Otto exclaimed.

"Lulu, sing something."

Lulu stretched out her neck and began to sing. "*Row, row, row your boat...*"

Otto started laughing. "That is so neat!"

Even I was impressed. Lulu was a knowledgeable bird! "Amazing, Lulu!" I cooed.

Lulu looked at me, amused, and winked.

"I taught her that one so that we can sing it as a round," Charlotte said. "She knows a few songs."

I could tell Otto was thinking about me then. "My Homer can't talk, but he's a great homing pigeon."

"What's that mean?"

"Well, you can take a homing pigeon far, far away and it can fly back, straight to where its home is. Homing pigeons know exactly where they're going, without a map. It's in their brains. Scientists think they use the sun and the landscape together as a compass."

"Cool. I didn't know that."

"They used to use homing pigeons to carry messages, like during wars and stuff."

"Wow!"

"Homer can fly home from miles away. I've timed him. Sometimes he even beats us home, and we're driving in a car."

"Who's 'us'?"

"My grandad and me. He had pigeons when he was a boy. The two of us built Homer's cage together."

"What about your parents? Are they okay with you having a pet bird?"

"I live with my grandad. It's just us." I felt Otto deflate some. I bet he was thinking about how sad Grandad felt losing the gold watch.

"Oh," Charlotte said. "He sounds nice, helping you with Homer and everything."

Otto straightened up a bit. "He's great. We're training Homer for a race."

"That's cool," Charlotte commented.

"Yeah, it is!" he replied. "We have to get him powered up for his race. I just went to the store to get him some food. A special mix that Mr. Petz makes just for Homer." Otto tickled my chin. "He's a very special bird." I could tell from his voice that he was proud.

"Yeah, I go to PetzGalore for Lulu's stuff. Food...toys. Lulu's pretty picky about what she eats."

"Homer likes most anything Mr. Petz mixes up."

Charlotte stroked Lulu's feathers. "I think Lulu and Homer should meet formally. Maybe they would like each other."

Otto grinned and gently stretched out his finger, an invitation for me to climb on.

"This, Homer, is the fabulous Lulu!" he said.

Lulu and I exchanged knowing glances.

"How do you do?" I cooed.

"How do you do?" Lulu squawked. "Is this crazy, or what?"

"So crazy!"

Charlotte was beside herself. "See?" she exclaimed. "I told you! Just listen to them jabber! They really like each other!"

"Aw, they're just squawking at each other," Otto replied. "They don't even speak the same language."

"How do you know?"

"Have you ever heard of a parrot speaking pigeon? That's ridiculous."

"Have you ever heard of a parrot *not* speaking pigeon?"

"Well, you got me there."

Lulu and I giggled. "If they only knew," I cooed.

"See?" Charlotte exclaimed again. "They are communicating! I can tell by the way they're looking at each other."

I could tell that Otto was dubious as he studied Lulu and me intently. "You really think so?"

"Definitely. They're going to be great friends. I can always tell these things."

Lulu and I continued to bob and nod, squawk and coo, putting on a show as Otto and Charlotte watched, entranced.

"They think we just met!" Lulu giggled.

"They think they've made some scientific break-through!" I added. We burst into a laughing convulsion of coos and squawks.

Charlotte clapped her hands, obviously delighted. "See? Isn't this great?" she exclaimed.

It looked like Otto was beginning to think Charlotte was right.

The two of us birds did feel right at home with each other, like we had been friends forever.

"Look at the way Homer is bobbing his head up and down!" Otto said.

Charlotte nodded. "And look how Lulu has spread out her tail feathers!"

Suddenly Charlotte glanced past Otto's shoulder and let out a shriek. "Hey! What is *that*?" She stood up and pointed to a dark form darting quickly into the bushes. "It's like a...*rat*!"

Lulu and I had been so busy showing off we hadn't noticed the rat's approach. We both puffed out our feathers in surprise and alarm just in time to see the dark form disappear lickety-split into the shadows.

"Ew! I think it *was* a rat." Charlotte grimaced. "That's disgusting!"

Just then she let out another shriek. "Hey! Where is my *hair clip*?" She frantically looked all around the park bench. "It was right here! And now it's gone! It's just gone!"

"I'm sure it must be around here somewhere," Otto said. He scoured the area around the bench.

Charlotte looked down her shirt and shook out her hair. "I just had it! I laid it on the bench just a second ago!"

It looked to me like Charlotte was about to cry. Several adults had gathered, but there was nothing anyone could do.

"I really loved that clip," Charlotte moaned. "I mean really *really*. I got it for my birthday. I loved it. Mom is going to kill me!"

I couldn't believe it. Yet another theft!

Lulu's expression was one of rankled astonishment. She looked at me squarely. "This involves me now too," she said. "And Charlotte. Whoever stole Charlotte's hair clip that she really loved—and I mean really *really* loved— answers to me."

Otto took one more glance around the area. "I'm sorry I have to go now, Charlotte. And I'm very sorry about your hair clip. I'll see you soon, though, okay?"

Charlotte looked so gloomy. "Okay. See you."

I thought for a moment. "Lulu, how about we meet here tomorrow? The newspaper says it's going to be a nice day...maybe Charlotte will bring you to the park."

"Sounds good," Lulu replied. Then she jerked with a start. "Wait a minute. What do you mean, 'the newspaper says it's going to be a nice day'?"

I cooed. "So, Lulu...you can speak Human? Well, I've got a surprise for you. I can *read* Human! See you tomorrow!"

CHAPTER NINE

The day was drizzly. Otto bounded up the steps to the loft with the newspaper and a cup of seed in hand. He spread out the paper and scattered some millet and cracked corn, then stopped to point to a small newspaper article in one corner. His expression was somber. "This is about Grandad's watch."

I could tell that Otto couldn't stop thinking about the stolen watch. Grandad had been melancholy, almost despondent since it had been taken. When they were up on the roof the two of them spoke of nothing else. Most of the time they were silent.

"Homer," he said. "I've got some errands to run for Grandad. Have your breakfast and you can come with me."

Otto carefully made my little spot on top of his cap. "First stop, post office," he said as we headed off, with him darting and hopping between puddles. "To buy stamps and mail Grandad's insurance form."

I heard Otto humming a little tune as he walked. Despite the loss of the watch and the upsetting neighborhood jewel thefts, it was good to be outside, riding on top of Otto's head. The warm summer drizzle felt refreshing, and I groomed and preened my feathers as I bobbed along.

And there was something to be happy about: my new friend Lulu. I wondered if maybe Otto would ever invite Charlotte and Lulu along when we went on one of my test flights, as observers.

I cooed with anticipation.

Otto bounded around a corner and ran into the back of someone in a pink rain poncho. I almost fell off my perch.

"Hey, watch where you're going—oh! Otto!" The pink poncho was Charlotte's, Lulu perched on her shoulder.

I couldn't see Otto's face, but I imagine it turned red.

"Sorry. I guess I wasn't looking."

"You guessed right." Charlotte checked to make sure Lulu was all right, and then looked up at me. "Hi, Homer," she said, stroking my neck feathers.

Otto pointed. "I was just going to get some stamps. The post office is right here."

Charlotte shook some of the wet off of her poncho. "Oh." She held up a paper bag. "I just got a toy for Lulu."

"Cool."

"Well, you want some company?"

"That'd be great." Otto opened the door of the post office for Charlotte.

They stood under the bored gaze of the post office clerk, poring over the sheets of stamps under the heavy glass countertop.

"Those are nice," Charlotte said, pointing to a sheet of garden flower stamps. "Or those, jazz musicians. Or those, the Everglades wildlife ones."

I watched Otto put his nose to the glass and eye the scenes from the Everglades, full of ibises and egrets and alligators. "That set!" he said to the clerk.

He paid for the sheet of stamps and mailed his grandad's insurance form, and then we ambled down the street. The drizzle was letting up, and patches of sky were visible between clumps of gray clouds.

Otto and Charlotte stood under a shop awning and examined the sheet of stamps through the tissue paper envelope.

"Hey, Homer," Lulu clucked. "What's all this you said about you being able to read Human? Explain!"

"Ah, yes," I replied. "Well, in a way it's a long story, but to make it short, I can read Human words."

"What do you mean, 'read Human words'?"

"Does Charlotte put papers on the bottom of your cage?"

"Yes. So?"

"Ever notice those little black marks all over the pages?"

"Yes, of course..."

"Those little black marks all over the sheets of paper mean different letters and words, to humans. It's one way humans communicate. They put the all the little marks in order and it helps them tell stories. They can actually say things to each other just by putting those marks on the paper."

"You mean there are little black marks for 'Lulu'?"

"Exactly!"

"Or 'hair clip'? Or 'I'm hungry'?"

"Yes! Those little black marks stand for words."

Lulu looked flabbergasted. "Interesting! Who'd have thought?"

"Well...are you ready for this? I can read them. I know what they mean."

Lulu gave a squawk.

"It started years ago. I found myself walking across

newspapers day after day. It wasn't long before I was piecing things together."

"How?"

"You know what a picture is? Or a photograph of something?"

"Yes. Charlotte has a photograph of me on the wall. Well, actually it's a photograph of both of us, but mostly me."

"Well, in the newspaper there are pictures, or photographs, or cartoons, and words that go along with them. After a while it all began to make sense to me. Now I can read newspapers...street signs...anything."

Lulu's eyes widened. "That's amazing, Homer!" she gushed. She gestured to a trash can a few meters from the bench that had writing on it. "What's that say?"

"Easy. 'Trash Only'."

Lulu gave a little squawk. Then she nodded at a nearby sign. "And that?"

"'Loitering Prohibited'."

"Wow!"

"Here's the thing. Even though I can read, I can't make Otto understand that. Well, not until now."

"Not until now *what*? What do you mean?"

"I mean you! You can be my translator."

"Translator?"

"I can read it, and you can speak it."

"Oh...I get it. You read something, tell me what it says, and I tell Charlotte, in Human."

"Exactly."

"But Homer, I only know a few words in Human. Hardly any at all. Just the ones that Charlotte has taught me, and believe me, they wouldn't be very useful."

"What do you mean?"

"'Grape'? 'Hair clip'? 'Pretty girl'?"

"That's okay. We'll figure it out. We just need to report the bare facts. They'll get the idea, and really quickly, I bet."

Lulu puffed up and ruffled her neck feathers in anticipation. "I can't wait to try this out."

"I can't either, but for right now, we're keeping an eye out for odd behavior in the park. Then we'll have something to tell Otto and Charlotte about. I'll be close by, within squawking distance!"

"Got it," Lulu squawked.

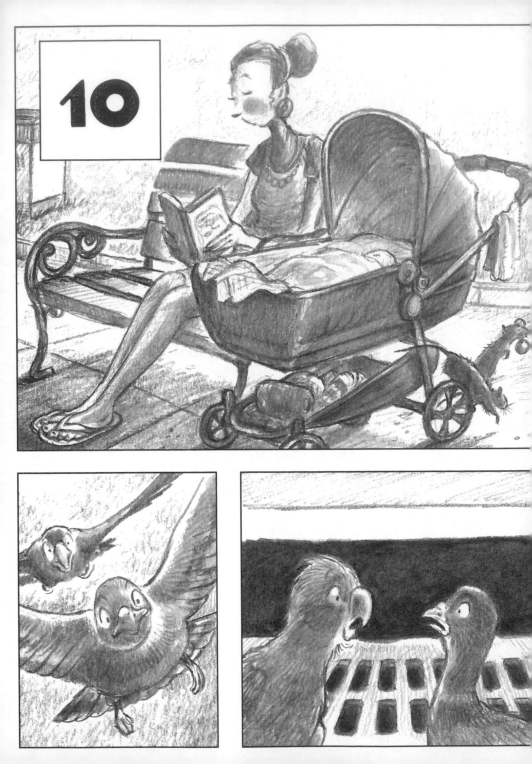

CHAPTER TEN

The next day I of course flew to the park. It seemed like if I was going to get anywhere in this investigation it would somehow involve the park. I kept thinking about Dick Tracy and what he would do. He'd investigate. He'd observe. He'd keep at it until he had a breakthrough.

I circled over the south end of the park. Down below I saw Carlos with some other city pigeons. I called down to him.

"Hey, Carlos! Anything to report?"

"Hey, Homer!" The group of pigeons looked up in unison. "We're forming a squad! Taking turns at different spots in the park, looking for suspicious characters, just like you said!"

I loved that he had recruited reinforcements. "Thanks, buddy! Keep me posted!"

Then I circled to the north end of the park and, sure enough, spotted Lulu and Charlotte, sitting on their favorite bench. I swooped down and settled on one end of the bench.

Charlotte was reading and didn't notice me come in for a landing.

"Good morning, Lulu. Keeping a lookout?"

"Morning, Homer. Yep. But nothing to report yet."

"Roger that," I said, using my Dick Tracy lingo. "I'm off for some surveillance."

After a short reconnaissance flight, I took a position sitting on top of a lamppost not far from Lulu's bench. It was a perfect observation point. I could see down several sidewalks in different directions.

The morning was clear and mild, a perfect-weather day, so pedestrian traffic was heavy. Several of Carlos's squad pigeons glided past, and I gave them a knowing nod.

"Gotcha covered, Homer!" one of them shouted.

Down on the sidewalk men and women passed by, dressed for business and clutching briefcases and bags. A boy rolled along on his skateboard. Joggers padded by, clutching water bottles.

A large yellow dog trotted past, pulling a man along on a leash.

Another man came by in a motorized cart, pulled an

overflowing garbage bag out of a trash can, replaced it with an empty bag, and then drove away.

Typical morning, I thought, and I yawned.

After a while a woman, her baby carriage loaded with all sorts of baby accoutrements, stopped at a park bench. She plopped onto the bench and sighed. I watched her take out a magazine and absently flip the pages while she rocked the carriage gently back and forth.

But then I noticed two shadows underneath the baby carriage.

My eyes popped and I gulped twice when I saw the pink nose of a gray rat poke out from behind one of the carriage wheels. Then the pink nose of another appeared.

The two rats sniffed the air and scanned the landscape. They scaled the wheels of the carriage, climbing up into it, then disappeared under the baby blanket.

That's when I saw the glint of something shiny in the carriage.

My feathers puffed out in excitement. The thieving rats were at it again!

I cooed loudly, agitated. The woman was still flipping the pages of her magazine, never noticing the nearly imperceptible movements under the blanket of the sleeping baby.

In a moment the rats emerged. Their eyes darted around as they slithered down to the sidewalk. One of them held a shiny silver baby rattle in its mouth.

I flapped and clucked, making a fuss. I didn't want to take my eyes off of the rats. "Lulu! LULU! Over here!"

"What is it, Homer?" Lulu squawked back from across the way.

"The rats! The *rats*! They're back! Come quickly!"

The two rats looked up at me on the lamppost in surprise. "What's with the lunatic pigeon? Let's beat it!" one of them squealed.

"*Yur sedd ihh!*" the one with the rattle in its mouth agreed. They quickly darted off down the sidewalk.

"Lulu!" I shouted. "Follow me!"

In a frenzied flap of feathers I took off after the rats, who were weaving and dodging in between human feet and dogs' legs. They scooted off to one side, across the grass and through a flower bed, and then onto Marion Street.

I glanced over my left wing and saw Lulu in the distance. With her clipped wing she was no match for my speed, but she pushed to keep up.

"I'm coming, Homer!" she called out.

We both heard Charlotte's frantic attempts to coax Lulu back.

"Lulu! No! Come back here! Lulu!" she screamed. "Somebody! Help! My bird flew away!"

The two rats scampered along the edge of the sidewalk, trying to hide in the overgrown grass and weeds and the shadow of the brick edging. But I never let them out of my sight.

They came to the edge of a storm drain and paused for just a second, which gave Lulu time to catch up. The sun glinted off of the silver rattle. They took one more look at Lulu and me before disappearing into the darkness beneath the street.

Lulu skidded onto the sidewalk and I landed beside her.

"If I hadn't seen it with my own eyes, I wouldn't have believed it," she squawked. "They stole that shiny thing?"

"Right in front of me."

"Well, what do we do now?"

"I'll follow them. I have to."

Lulu looked at the dark storm drain. She gulped. "Down *there?*"

"What else can I do?" I replied. "How else can we catch these crooks?"

We shuffled to the edge of the drain opening and peered down into the darkness.

"Uh...I don't know about this, Homer," Lulu gulped. "It's dark and creepy down there. Are you sure this is a good idea? I mean, you don't know where you're going, or even what to look for when you're down in that stinky place."

I gulped too. "I figure...well, I figure I'll figure that out as I go. And when I find where the gold pocket watch is hidden, I'll nab it...and then get out of there fast."

"What about the hair clip that Charlotte really, really loves?"

"I'll nab that too."

"What if you don't find anything?"

"But I will!"

"Right after you get lost forever and ever. It's dark and creepy!"

"You forget one thing: I'm a homing pigeon!"

"I'm beginning to think Charlotte's hair clip isn't worth this." We heard Charlotte wailing in the distance. "And she's about to lose her mind with me taking off like this."

"There's more to this than a hair clip."

Lulu paused. "You're right, Homer. There is more to this. I love Charlotte. And you love Otto, and Grandad. And they love us. We can do this."

"*We?*"

"Yep. I'm in this too." Off in the park, Charlotte's cries continued. "Look, I have to get back to her. How about this: want to meet tonight?"

"And explore under the street then?"

"Yes. But remember, I'm not so great at flying around. In fact, I've never flown at night."

"We'll fly together. It'll be fine. I'll come to your house tonight. Let's say...when the clock dongs once. Sound good?"

"Okay."

"Which apartment building is yours?"

"You know the yellow brick one? With the guy dressed in red standing out front all day long? Right on the park?"

"I know the building."

"That's the one."

"Which apartment is yours?"

"Second floor. Left side of the building. Charlotte's mother has scads of plants and flowers on the balcony. You can't miss it. Charlotte's window is the one nearest the balcony. It's one of those slidey kinds of windows. I can open it no problem."

I nodded. "Okay, then we're all set. I'll see you tonight."

Lulu gave a nervous squawk. "This whole thing is crazy, but okay. I'll calm down, I promise."

We heard the frantic cries of Charlotte as she scoured the trees, sky, and power lines, calling for her beloved Lulu.

I gestured toward Charlotte. "Right, now go calm *her* feathers."

That night I glided silently through the dark city streets, then across Keeler Park to Van Clive Street. Lulu's yellow brick apartment building glowed under the bright streetlights. It felt a little creepy and strange to be out at night. This wasn't a test flight and I wasn't under the care and safety of Otto and Grandad.

I perched on one of streetlights. On the left side of the building, on the second floor, were *two* balconies full of plants.

"Oh, brother," I mumbled. "Which one?"

I flapped as quietly as I could to one of them.

With a soft rush of feathers I landed on the railing. Chairs with flowered cushions and a jungle of plants in pots filled the balcony. I noticed the window nearest to me was already cracked open. I glided to the sill.

Luckily it was the right apartment. Lulu was already at the open window and cautiously crept to the ledge outside. Her large claws scraped at the metal frame.

"Shh!" I whispered.

"Shh yourself," Lulu whispered back.

"Let's go."

Lulu pushed the sliding glass window open some more to wiggle her body through. The window frame squeaked a little, like tiny nails on a chalkboard.

"Hey! Who's that?" came Charlotte's groggy voice through the dark. "Lulu? Is that you?"

Lulu shot me a glance and then made snoring sounds, slow and even, like she was in a deep sleep.

We heard Charlotte turn over under her comforter. In a few moments all was quiet.

"That's a relief," I said. "We'll be back before Charlotte knows you're gone."

Lulu tiptoed over the windowsill and made a short, silent glide to one of the flowered cushions.

We gave each other a nod and then headed out into the night.

CHAPTER ELEVEN

In a few minutes we landed in front of the Marion Street storm drain.

Lulu stared down into the dark drain. "Homer, once we go down there, we're looking for stolen treasure, right?"

"Right."

"All sorts of stolen goodies, right?"

"Right."

"Everything just sitting there waiting for us to find it, right?"

"Huh?"

"Exactly! It is very hard for me to imagine stolen treasure just sitting there...without some*one* or maybe *more* than one someone guarding it."

"What do you mean?"

"Cats! Rats! Who knows what else? They've gone to a lot of trouble to steal this stuff; maybe they'll go to a lot of trouble to protect it!"

"You're right, Lulu."

"And how do we find it, to begin with?" She glanced nervously again down the storm drain. "Down...*there!*"

She had me there. I didn't know, exactly. But I remembered Dick Tracy saying *"Any clue is a good clue."*

"We're looking for signs. For clues. This is exploratory. We have to start somewhere."

"I'll say it one more time," Lulu groaned. "This whole idea is crazy."

"Do you want to stay behind? You made the decision to come along."

"I don't want to be the chicken!"

"Then come on." With that, I glided down into the inky darkness into the storm drain.

Lulu hesitated, then followed.

Deep under the city streets we followed along the damp walls of the labyrinth, first taking a right into a side tunnel, then a left into another tunnel, then another left into yet another tunnel. I didn't know which way to go as we looked for clues, but I felt that my homing instinct would lead us out, regardless. Besides the small dim electric lights that glowed from the walls, there was a pale glow from the streetlights above that filtered through the manhole covers and storm drains, faintly lighting our way...but only faintly. The passageways got narrower and darker as we ventured farther and farther underground. The atmosphere became danker and mustier, thick with the stale smell of unventilated, motionless air.

We flew as silently as possible, keeping our wingbeats to a minimum, gliding when we could. I was a little worried about Lulu's clipped wing, but she was a champ and kept at it.

We stopped at intervals to rest and listen, hoping for clues.

Deeper and deeper we went. Lulu eyes were wide in the near darkness. "Homer...are you sure we'll be able to find our way out of here?" she whispered.

I felt I needed to be reassuring, even if I didn't feel completely confident. "Easy. Can do," I whispered back. "Remember? With me it's instinctive. How's your left wing?"

"It's okay. I can do this." She clacked her mandibles anxiously, but we continued on our way through the tunnels.

We had taken a seemingly endless series of left and right turns. I was beginning to wonder if we had made a mistake in coming underground, and I wondered if my homing instincts were good enough to pull us out of the tunnels after all. I was considering turning back when we both noticed a faint yellow glow up ahead.

I nodded at the dim light. Lulu nodded back, and we flew as silently as we could to a stone ledge.

The ledge overlooked a large, cavernous room. The walls and sloping ceiling of the room were made of tightly fitted stones, old and slippery looking. A dim, eerie, flickering light came from a few ages-old electric lights that were suspended on the walls.

The room widened to form a large gallery crowded with an array of scraggly-looking rats and cats.

I was surprised to recognize two of the rats. I whispered to Lulu. "It's them!"

"Who?"

"The rats that stole the doggie collars." I noticed they were wearing the jeweled collars...and one of them carried the silver baby's rattle.

Our eyes followed the two rats as they crept nervously up several steps to a stone platform.

Suddenly Lulu's eyes bugged out and her crest feathers stood straight up.

My own feathers ruffled in astonishment.

There, beneath one of the old-fashioned lights, sat an alligator.

She was huge. Her long tail curved and draped heavily across the dank floor. Her skin, bumpy and thick, was like armor. She glowered menacingly at everyone in the gallery, her yellow-green eyes catching the light as she delicately stroked her pale throat with the sides of her giant claws.

She was covered in ornaments. A glittering tiara perched on her knotty head. Her short arms were thick with bracelets and bangles and watches. Festoons of necklaces, dotted with precious gems, hung from her neck. Spread out on the stones around her were small piles of treasures: rings and jeweled combs, earrings and stickpins, cigarette cases and jeweled lipstick tubes, compacts and small mirrors with gilt frames, and a sea of cuff links. Even in the dim light the sapphires and diamonds and garnets and all the other jewels sent thousands of tiny colored sparkles twinkling across the stone walls and ceiling.

One of the rats crawled forward. He spit out the silver baby rattle. "Here, Snaps," he squeaked, barely above a whisper. "A small token." Then he nervously placed one of the jeweled doggie collars at the massive feet of the alligator. "Behold! Amethysts!"

The alligator looked bored. "Is that all?" she growled.

The second rat scurried up with the second collar. "And this, Snaps!" he peeped hopefully. "Emeralds! And it says Genuine Cowhide on the inside!"

The giant gator yawned. "Been there, done that," she sighed, but then she picked up the two collars and squeezed each one onto a toe.

Lulu couldn't help herself and gave a little squawk.

My heart skipped a beat. "Shh!" I whispered. "Don't give us away!"

"Sorry," Lulu whispered back. "But I've never seen so much...*much*!"

"I know...look at all that loot! Now we know where all of those stolen things have been going." We both stared, mesmerized, as the huge alligator wrapped a long strand of pearls around her wrist while a black-and-brown tabby sat at her feet, polishing her toenails. Several other cats were bringing in more treasures and laying them at the gator's feet.

The giant reptile picked up a gilt mirror and studied her reflection. "Hmm," she growled. "Needs more red. More rubies! More *garnets*! And don't forget I like *sequins*!"

Several rat attendants scurried in different directions.

"Yes, Snaps!" one of them squeaked. "More rubies! Snaps wants more rubies!"

"And garnets!" another squealed as they raced off down different dark tunnels to search and steal from the humans on the streets above.

I looked at Lulu. "It's ordering everybody around." I whispered. "They do its bidding."

"What *is* it?"

"It's an alligator. I've seen pictures of them in books that Otto has," I whispered. "But never one this big. And its name must be Snaps. It's the mastermind...but it's hoarding all of this fancy stuff. I wonder why?"

Lulu glanced around nervously. "I don't know," she whispered back. "But maybe now that we've found where everything is going, we should get out of here. Let's vamoose. We'll figure this out, but up in the fresh air."

My instincts came in handy on the long trip back, and the two of us silently meandered and twisted our way through the long, convoluted tunnel. Soon we were back at the storm drain at the park.

The sun was just beginning to turn the sky pink. "Let's figure out a plan," I said after we were again breathing in the open air. "We need to stop this pack of thieves!"

Lulu painfully stretched out her clipped wing. Flapping and gliding through the tunnel had pushed her limits. "Homer, we need help," Lulu said. "We can't solve this without humans."

"Agreed. But how can we let them know what's going on so we can stop it?"

CHAPTER TWELVE

It was close, but I got back to my rooftop cage just before Otto came up to deliver my breakfast. All I could do that morning was sit on the wall of the rooftop, thinking of the reptilian colossus Lulu and I had seen in the sewer system below the city. Had there really been an alligator, covered in jewels? It seemed like a dream.

I was worn out after the night in the tunnels. I slept most of the afternoon and woke up hearing evening church bells off in the distance. I had even missed meal-time! Otto must have thought it strange that I didn't rouse myself for that. I saw that he had left my dinner millet and cracked corn for me.

I gazed down at Otto's window. The light was on, so I knew he was probably reading a *Dick Tracy* comic.

If only I could find some way to give him a clear message, I thought. *There must be something I could do....maybe from the inside?*

A moment later I swooped down to the sill.

Otto's desk light was on, but no one was in the room.

The window was cracked open. I slipped in.

I had been in Otto's room before, just a few times when the weather was truly nasty out or when Otto wanted some company. But I'd never been inside *alone* before...it felt kind of creepy. And I definitely felt a little sneaky.

I looked around for something I could use to communicate with Otto. There were books on a shelf, the desk and lamp, clothes scattered around, and a sports calendar on the wall, but nothing seemed useful to me as a way of giving Otto some sort of message.

But I noticed that the bedroom door was open. I glided over to it and skidded lightly across the slippery wooden floor to the threshold.

I peeked around the corner. There was another open door down the hall. I flapped to it.

In that room were another desk, another lamp, and more books. I flew to the desk, landing with a swoosh of feathers against papers.

Something caught my eye.

Brightly colored animals and plants figured prominently on a sheet of paper. It was the sheet of stamps Otto had purchased at the post office. The stamps depicted different kinds of colored birds and flowers—and an *alligator*! It looked just like Snaps!

It was a start. Maybe I could make Otto see the connection. I pecked at and peeled the adhesive-backed stamps. A Butterfly Orchid stamp stuck to my toes and I kicked it off. A Roseate Spoonbill stamp stuck to my beak and I had to shake my head vigorously to detach it. After much pecking and tearing and peeling, I finally had the American Alligator stamp I needed. "Success!" I cooed loudly.

My heart was doing little flips. This would definitely catch Otto's attention. He would see the obvious message in the alligator stamp, surely! I flew back to Otto's room, back to the windowsill, and out into the evening air.

Tomorrow morning there would be a stamp next to my food dish, and I would begin to show Otto what we were up against.

Otto was giving me my millet-corn-peanut breakfast when he stopped abruptly and stared at my dish.

"Wha—?" he stuttered. Then he stared at me. All I could do was look back and coo hopefully.

Just then we heard Grandad plodding up the stairs.

Otto carefully picked up the stamp. "Grandad, look at this. This was on Homer's food dish this morning."

Grandad looked at the stamp. "That's one of the new stamps. How'd it wind up here?"

"Beats me!"

"It's sticky. Maybe it got stuck to Homer's foot somehow when you were at the post office yesterday." Then Grandad paused. "But my desk was a mess this morning... and the stamps were everywhere. Can't figure it. Hmm." He checked on my cage and glanced at the sky, then headed back down the stairs.

Argh! No one was paying any attention to my obvious alligator stamp message!

But Otto hadn't quite given up. He carefully lifted me to his cap. "Breakfast will have to wait, Homer. Let's go find Charlotte. For some reason I want to show her your stamp."

We hurried down the stairs to the street. As luck would have it, we saw Charlotte coming down Donovan Street, enjoying a guava Danish.

"Okay," he said to her. "Take a look at what Homer left for me and tell me what you think of it." He held up the sticky stamp. "*This* was stuck to Homer's food dish this morning."

"Hey, isn't that one we got? It's an Everglades stamp, right?"

"Yep."

"And it was on Homer's food dish this morning? On the roof!"

"Yep."

"That is weird."

"When I showed it to Grandad, he told me his desk and stamps were messed up. No one else was up at the loft except Homer. Don't you think that's a little...nuts?"

"You think Homer left it for you?"

"Yes! I do!"

"How could he do that?"

"*Why* would he do that? A postage stamp with an alligator on it?"

I watched Charlotte study the stamp. Then I saw one corner of her mouth creep up in a funny smile. "Yeah, it's a little nuts, all right," she answered. "It's one of the *alligator* Everglades stamps." She looked at Homer and then spoke quietly and deliberately to Otto. "Otto, I don't want you to freak out. *Please* don't freak out. But..."

"But what?"

"Lulu keeps saying 'alligator.'"

"You're kidding me."

"No, I'm not. It's driving me crazy. And 'snaps.' She keeps saying 'snaps.' Over and over. I gave her a gingersnap but she spit it out. I gave her snap peas and she totally ignored them. I danced around the room snapping my fingers and she stared at me like I was a lunatic. I've never taught her the word 'snaps'. She's never said 'snaps' before, or 'alligator' either, for that matter, and now she's saying them all the time. It's making me a *crazy* person."

"Holy cow."

"And now *this*."

Charlotte reached into her cargo shorts pocket. "Lulu brought me this just this morning. I stuck it into my pocket without thinking much about it. But now..."

She handed Otto a rubber bath toy. A squeezy, water-squirting kind of bath toy. It was a green and yellow alligator.

I cooed with delight. Lulu was planting messages too!

Otto looked at Charlotte with surprise.

Charlotte nodded. "An alligator."

"You're kidding me."

Otto glanced again at the postage stamp. "Hmm. Either it's a really weird coincidence, or...they're trying to tell us something," Otto said. He reached up and gave me a pat. "Has Lulu ever done anything like this before? I know Homer hasn't."

"No! And *alligators*? What's the deal?"

"I only wish I spoke Bird. Then we could ask *them* what the deal is!"

"Now that you mention it, Lulu hasn't ever talked so much before. After she met Homer she got more verbal without me asking her to. She's talking all the time now. I can't get her to keep quiet."

"And Homer keeps tearing out pieces of the newspaper and bringing them to my windowsill. Look at this." He reached into his back pocket and pulled out a newspaper clipping. *The* newspaper clipping. The photograph of two distraught poodles that I had ripped out. "Homer came to my window the other night waving this around. He seemed so crazy about it. I thought it was strange. Can it be there's a connection somehow?"

I was so excited I cooed and bobbed for all I was worth.

Charlotte looked at me and caught her breath. "Yes, a connection...like he's building a nest or something! Maybe he and Lulu want to get married!"

I rolled my eyes and cooed in despair.

Otto looked at Charlotte and grunted. "Are you nuts? Two different species can't get married. It's against the law or something."

Charlotte ignored him. "I think we should put them together and see what happens."

Otto thought a moment. "Well...maybe that's not such a bad idea. They might give us an idea of what they're thinking. Why don't you bring Lulu up to the rooftop? We can monitor them and look for...anything unusual. At the very least they might give us another clue."

"This could be big!" Charlotte said. "Interspecies communication!"

Charlotte took off down the street toward her apartment. Otto and I made a beeline back to the rooftop.

CHAPTER THIRTEEN

As it happens, the newspaper that day ran a story on another jewel theft, but not in Keeler Park this time.

PARK THEFTS CONTINUE

Visitors to Addison Park have seen an increase in petty theft over the past few days. Residents are warned to keep possessions close at hand at all times. This comes after weeks of crime in Keeler Park.

I tugged and ripped the article out of the newspaper. I wanted another clipping to show Otto. And just when I was at my rippiest and tuggiest, Otto came bounding up the rooftop steps. I tore the article out and proudly picked it up with my beak.

He stared at me. "Homer, what are you *up* to?"

But he read the clipping. "You are *definitely* trying to tell me something, Homer. This isn't some crazy random newspaper shredding habit you've got, I just know it. It's *you* giving *me* a message."

I gave Otto an encouraging coo!

We heard Grandad shout from the bottom of the stairs up to the roof. "Otto! You've got company!"

Lulu clung to Charlotte's shoulder as the two came up the loft steps. "Hi, Homer!" she squawked. "We're here! Finally!"

I paced back and forth across the landing platform, excited.

"Look, Charlotte," Otto said. "Homer did another crazy thing! He tore out this article from the paper. Read this and tell me it isn't a message. It's about the latest thefts."

Charlotte read the article silently.

I was about to bust open. I cooed loudly.

"He's telling us something," Charlotte said at last. "Most definitely."

I looked at Lulu. "Now they're getting it!" I bobbed up and down. "See, Lulu? I found another clue to show them! A story about another jewel theft. This time over in Addison Park."

"Addison Park?"

"It's like I read in *Dick Tracy*. After thieves steal too much in one area, they move to another. My theory is that that Snaps is enlarging her territory, including more parks. Maybe Keeler Park isn't as worthwhile as it used to be, and Snaps is branching out into other places around the city."

"Maybe with so many newspaper articles about the thefts, humans are more careful with their stuff."

"That's a lot of news to get across to Otto and Charlotte," I said.

Lulu spread her wings and tail feathers. "Great!" she squawked. "We have a lot to tell them. Let's get this newscast going!"

With that, Lulu began parading up and down the rooftop deck, squawking and raising her crest feathers. I fell in step behind her, cooing and bobbing.

Otto and Charlotte stared, mouths agape.

Lulu flapped to the porch railing and began speaking Human.

"*Alligator! Alligator! Alligator!*" she squawked.

"See? She's at it again!" Charlotte exclaimed. "Again with the alligator talk."

"Yeah...great! Get her to keep speaking," Otto said. "But I'm going to write down everything." He grabbed his pencil and clipboard. "Don't let me miss a word."

"Well, start with 'alligator,'" Charlotte said.

"*Alligator!*" Lulu squawked again. "*Watch!*"

Otto and Charlotte stared at the parrot.

"She said 'watch,'" Otto gasped. "Plain as day."

"She sure did," Charlotte replied. "Write it down!"

Otto scribbled furiously.

"*Watch!*" repeated Lulu. "*Alligator!*"

Otto looked aggravated, then doubtful. "Do you think maybe she's just spouting gibberish?"

"Could be," replied Charlotte. "But it's really a coincidence that she's saying 'watch,' with your Grandad's watch being stolen and all.'"

I fluttered with frustration. "Say it again, Lulu," I suggested.

Lulu stretched out her neck and screeched, "*Watch! Alligator!*"

"They're trying to tell us something, I just know it," Otto said. "Something important."

"Try another word," I said. "Say 'hair clip.'"

"*Hair clip!*" Lulu shrieked.

Otto and Charlotte stared at each other. "Write it down, Otto!" Charlotte squealed.

"*Alligator! Hair clip!*" Lulu screeched again.

"How about 'jewel thieves'?" I said.

Lulu let out with a strident *"Jewel thieves!"*

Charlotte's eyes popped. "Write it down! 'Jewel thieves'!"

Lulu looked at me hopefully. "I think we're getting somewhere," she squawked.

"How about 'underground,' Lulu?" I clucked.

"Underground!" squawked Lulu.

Otto sucked in his breath. "Wait just a second! The newspaper article! The one that Homer brought to my windowsill—it was about the jewel thefts at Keeler Park!"

"Do you think they're trying to tell us about a jewel theft?" Charlotte gasped. "There has to be a connection!"

Otto laughed excitedly. "Nah...that can't be. That's too crazy!"

"Underground!" Lulu squawked again.

"Huh? 'Underground'?" Charlotte asked. "She's saying 'underground'...but I don't understand what that could mean. Maybe underground like the subway? Maybe the jewel thieves are making their getaways using the subway!"

"No!" Lulu squawked. *"Jewels! Underground!"*

I was vexed. "I don't think they're getting it."

But just then Otto slapped his hand against his forehead.

"Wait! I just remembered something else! The newspaper article mentioned something about 'underground'...the police said the thefts might be part of an underground ring. 'Underground'! Like secret, like gangsters!"

I flapped over to land near Otto's feet and cooed in frustration.

Charlotte pointed at him. "I think you've got something, Otto. Look how excited Homer got when you said that!"

"Homer!" Lulu screeched. "The only thing we can do is to try to get them to follow us. Let's show them where to go!" She flapped toward the wooden steps, and I followed her down.

Charlotte gasped, pointing at us. "Look! They're leading us somewhere! I just know it! They *want* us to follow them!"

"Let's go!" Otto whooped. Charlotte picked up Lulu and carried her protectively, and the three of them raced down the stairs to the street, with me flapping and gliding in the lead.

Lulu flew out of Charlotte's arms and landed on the pavement next to me. Otto and Charlotte stared in stunned silence as we hopped and leaped and fluttered our wings in front of the storm drain.

"*Alligator! Jewel thieves!*" Lulu screeched. "*Hair clip! Underground!*"

"Oh my gosh," Charlotte groaned finally. "You don't think they mean underground as in down *there?*"

"They must," Otto said. "This has gotta be the place. They're telling us that this is where the jewel thieves are." He looked around. "It's the storm drain nearest the corner of Donovan and Marion." He took out his pad and pencil and jotted some notes, looking grim. "We'll have to go down there if we want to figure out what this is all about."

Charlotte looked at Otto and said with anxiety, "*Us?* I'm not going to crawl down into that little space. We can't even fit!"

Otto pointed to a manhole cover a short distance away. "I bet that manhole drops into the same tunnel as this storm drain. We'll use that."

"Can't we just tell the police or somebody about what's happening?"

"You really think they'd listen to a couple of kids and their pet birds? Ha!"

"I really, really, really think we need to tell a grown-up."

"Like they'd believe us."

"But if we explained everything and then—"

"Oh, yeah?" Otto interrupted. "Explained? Explained that our birds were telling us giving us information about the jewel thefts? They'd think we were nuts. No, this is for us to figure out on our own." He grinned. "I think we can. Don't you?"

I saw Charlotte hesitate, but then she smiled back. "Well, this just sounds so *crazy*. But I'm game...if you are...I guess."

I guess we had made our point. "Let's get these guys back," Otto laughed. "Tomorrow is Sunday. The street will be empty, with only a few people around. We'll go down the manhole then."

"It's going to be dark down there. We'll need supplies and stuff."

Otto nodded as he lifted me off the sidewalk and onto his cap. "We'll need flashlights."

"And maybe we can find a map of the underground sewer system somewhere."

"Good idea. We can both check."

Charlotte took Lulu onto her arm, stroking her neck feathers. "Should we wear disguises?"

"Huh?"

"I mean, maybe we don't want to look like ourselves. So the thieves don't recognize us after."

Otto pondered this. "Wear something dark. We'll blend in. We'll go undetectable instead of unrecognizable."

"Got it. Tomorrow morning? How about seven a.m.?"

"Roger that."

CHAPTER FOURTEEN

On Saturday afternoon Otto had stopped by the library. When he got back to check on my water dish he was talking—to me I guess, but also to himself—about the research he had done. He had found a rather basic map of the sewage and drainage system for his neighborhood and had a copy made. I saw him replace the batteries in his mini flashlight, which he shoved into his belly pack alongside several granola bars.

Very early Sunday morning, he spread out the newspaper and gave me a quick breakfast. "You gotta eat kinda fast this morning, Homer," he said as he scattered the cracked corn and millet. "We have places to go!" He positioned me on his cap, and we tiptoed past Grandad's bedroom. Otto left a note on the kitchen table. "See you later, XO" was all it said. Then he grabbed a juice box out of the refrigerator before creeping quickly but silently out the front door.

The morning was hot and sticky and it felt like it might

rain. We headed down the street and crossed through Keeler Park. Charlotte and Lulu were already waiting for us; Charlotte had on a dark blue jacket with a big pocket that held a penlight and a baggie of M&Ms.

"We must be out of our minds," she mumbled as Otto and I came up the sidewalk. She looked up at the brightening sky. "Well, at least it's going to be an unbearable day. Perfect for getting lost forever under the city."

Otto grinned. "I've got a map; we've got flashlights. We're going to solve the mystery of the neighborhood jewel thefts and be heroes. We'll be in all the newspapers. You'll see."

"Yeah, we'll be in all the newspapers, all right. On the obituaries page."

We crossed the park to Donovan Street. Sunday meant less traffic, and the oppressive, humid air meant few pedestrians. I could tell Otto was relieved to find that his prediction had been correct: there were hardly any people on Donovan.

We quickly reached the manhole. Otto put his fingers into the holes and pulled. I nearly toppled off his head, but I hung on tightly.

"Oof!" Otto groaned. "This thing weighs about a million pounds. Here, help me pull."

Charlotte planted Lulu on the sidewalk, and I swooped down to her side.

"Oh, brother! You're not kidding!" Charlotte grumbled as they struggled, dragging the heavy iron cover off to one side. Then they let go and it dropped with a loud clang.

Otto looked around. "Hope nobody heard that."

Charlotte peered down into the dark, drippy depths below. "Do you think it's okay, Otto? I mean, it's pretty icky-looking down there."

I looked at Lulu. "They ain't seen nothin' yet!"

Lulu gave a little squawk of agreement.

"Yeah, it's darker than I thought it'd be," Otto said.

"Suddenly this whole thing seems like a wild goose chase. I mean, we're following a hunch just because Lulu and Homer are acting crazy."

"But suppose the hunch is a good one? How else are we going to find the mastermind behind the jewel thefts?"

"Well...I guess. Still, do you think it's safe? How far down does it go?"

"There's only one way to find out. We wait until no one is looking, then we...go down."

Otto and Charlotte looked up and down Donovan Street. There was a man busy sweeping the street in front of his frozen yogurt shop, but he took no notice of them. Otherwise the street was empty. The park was still quiet.

"Now," Otto said. "Come on, Homer." He lifted me to his cap. He swung his legs over the edge of the manhole and dangled his feet blindly around until they found the top rung of the metal ladder. "Here goes nothing," he said, climbing down.

Charlotte put Lulu on her shoulder and followed us down. No one saw us slip into the inky darkness below.

CHAPTER FIFTEEN

At first it seemed pitch-black before our eyes adjusted to the gloom. "I think we'd better use just one flashlight at a time," Otto said. "There's no telling how long the batteries'll last."

Charlotte looked alarmed. "You turn yours off. I want mine *on*."

The two of them pored over the map Otto had copied from the library, tracing the flashlight beam along the colorful tunnels and channels and corridors. "Which way?" Charlotte asked.

I saw Otto hesitate. He seemed a little overwhelmed. The inside of an underground city tunnel was dark. And drippy. And daunting.

He looked at me. "Homer will know the way, right? Which way, Homer?"

Just the lead I was hoping for. I was pretty sure I knew where to go.

I flapped my way down the tunnel, the same one Lulu and I had first explored.

"Okay! This way. He wants us to go this way." Otto looked a little relieved to have someone else in charge. He and Charlotte, with Lulu still clutching her shoulder, started to follow me down the narrow tunnel, gravitating toward each next little patch of light that filtered through from the storm drains high above us.

I'd fly a short distance, then wait for them to catch up. As I led them through the tunnel, Otto tried to follow our route on the rudimentary map he had printed out. But it looked like it was becoming increasingly difficult to decipher in the darkness.

Otto was getting frustrated. "This can't be right. There are a lot more tunnels down here than this map is showing. Look: if we're *here*, then I think we should take the next tunnel on the left."

"Why?" Charlotte asked. "We don't even know where we're going. I thought Homer was leading the way. How can you even guess where to go?"

To be honest, in that labyrinth of tunnels I was less sure of myself than I thought I'd be.

And also to be honest, I wasn't sure what information Otto was going to glean from the map he was clutching. I think it was more of a comfort for him than an actual navigational aid.

Lulu and I had found Snaps's lair mostly by accident. I could find our way out, but I wasn't sure I could find Snaps again. Now I was the one hesitating.

"Homer seems a little confused," Otto said. "See how he's backtracking?"

Charlotte nodded. "Do you think we're lost?"

"We're not lost...exactly."

"Maybe we should head back. I think your map is useless. And Homer is looking lost too! We're getting nowhere, and slowly."

"And maybe it's about time for a granola bar."

"Homer, are we near where the alligator is?" squawked Lulu.

I had to be honest. "Not sure. I think so. But it might be good to rest a minute."

Otto and Charlotte stood in the dim light of a drain. Otto looked up at the opening high above. "I think it's getting darker," he said.

The two of them ate their snacks, feeding bits of granola bar to Lulu and to me, with Otto trying to hold the flashlight at the same time.

"Would you please not shine that in my eyes?" Charlotte groused.

"Okay then, here, you hold it," Otto said.

We heard a rumble.

Charlotte gave a start and almost dropped her M&Ms. "What was that?"

"I don't know."

"Thunder," Lulu said to me.

"Yep, and thunder means storm. Sounds like a real doozie," I replied. Just as I had feared: the day had started out so hot and humid, I had thought a storm would be brewing at some point. And this sounded like a big one.

There was another rumble, and this time we all noticed a small flash at the drain opening from the lightning outside. I glanced at Lulu, a little uneasy.

"Thunderstorm?" Otto guessed.

"We'll be okay down here, though, right, Otto?" Charlotte asked him.

"Yeah, sure...I think so. We're out of the rain down here. But we should keep going."

We continued down the tunnel with me leading the way, gliding and stopping, gliding and stopping. As we went along, there were more faint flashes from various openings in the ceiling high above, and we heard more rumbles and the crackling of thunder.

I looked at Lulu; her yellow eyes looked jittery and tense when the lightning flashes illuminated them. I cooed to her reassuringly, but I knew my nerves were showing through.

Charlotte stopped. "Hey. Have you noticed something? Our feet are wet." She pointed the flashlight at her toes.

Otto looked around. "Yeah. So?"

"So...they weren't a minute ago." She shone the light across the floor of the tunnel. "It's wet in here. Let's go another way."

I saw that they were now standing in a shallow river. Otto and Charlotte turned and made their way down another tunnel, but then we heard the sound of trickling water ahead.

Otto got out his flashlight. "It's wet all around. And I think it's getting wetter. Look."

Water poured down in a ring from around the rim of a manhole cover high above us, sprinkling down in a mini rainstorm. The dull roar of the rain got louder.

"It must really be coming down outside," Charlotte said. Her flashlight pointed up and down the tunnel. "See? Water's dripping down from everywhere now."

"Yeah."

The pounding rain and crackling lightning increased. Piercing booms of thunder echoed down the tunnel. I could imagine the city above us being buffeted with bursts of wind, rocking and tossing the trees in Keeler Park. Small rivers must have been gushing down the streets before pouring through the storm drains around us.

The water was nearly up to Charlotte's knees. "Otto, I'm getting scared!" she shouted. "Look how high the water has gotten—and so quickly."

Otto looked worried too. "Charlotte," he called out over the din of the rain. "The tunnels all look the same! I can't tell where we've been or which route to take."

I had to admit I felt the same way.

The sound of rushing, splashing, pouring water echoed off the stone walls.

"I...I think we'd better try and find our way out!" Otto shouted.

"Agreed!" Charlotte called back. "But where? With all this water pouring in from the drains and the manholes...I don't think we can!" The rain pouring from above matted their hair and soaked their clothes. Lulu and I shook the water off, better prepared with our water-resistant feathers.

The storm pounded the city.

CHAPTER SIXTEEN

Otto and Charlotte floundered through the gray-brown water. The rushing sound was almost deafening. Charlotte's baggie of M&M's was a multicolored, watery mess. She stumbled and dropped her flashlight, which was carried away by the rolling current.

"Otto! I am *soaked*! This is *so gross*! When we get out of this—*if* we get out of this—I'm going to *kill* you!" Charlotte bellowed.

"You're as much to blame as me!" Otto yelled back.

"Me?"

"Yes! And anyway, I didn't know it was going to pour down like this."

Lulu shook her wet feathers and shivered. "Homer!" she squawked. "This isn't working. Can you find your way home?"

My internal compass was being tested like never before. I was underground—with no sun, no moon, no landscape—and the twisting underground tunnels were very disorienting. Seeing Otto, Charlotte, and Lulu in such distress made me anxious and a little muddled, but something inside my brain was clicking. Somehow, I knew which way to go.

"Which way, Otto? Which way?" Charlotte shouted. "I think this was a big mistake! I *gladly* give up my hair clip as lost forever."

"We've come this far, we might as well keep going," he said.

"We may end up washed out to sea!"

"Not with Homer. We gotta trust him. He knows his way back home from anywhere." Otto glanced down the beam of his flashlight. "I'm following Homer."

"*What?* For all we know he's just flying down the tunnel, as lost as we are. I think we should head back. We're getting nowhere slowly."

I flew to the right, down the dripping, flooding tunnel. Lulu followed.

"Lulu! Come back here!" Charlotte yelled.

Lulu kept up her wingbeats right beside me. "You know where you're going?" she screeched.

"You bet!" I called back. "We're not far now!"

Homer pointed with his flashlight. "Look! Homer is leading us up this tunnel! Yeah! It looks lighter up that way! What a good boy! Now we'll figure things out. Homer'll know the way!"

"It doesn't seem like it!" Charlotte shouted.

"We're heading the right way!" Otto responded. "I'd bet anything! Homer knows! He never gets lost!"

Otto and Charlotte waded after Lulu and me. The rumbles of thunder and pounding rain above had subsided and we could hear the muffled vibrations of a city bus on the street overhead.

Things were looking more and more familiar. I led them on through the maze of tunnels, murky and dripping. Otto and Charlotte kept close to the walls, where the pathway sloped up and the water wasn't as deep.

And then suddenly I knew just where we were. I took a sharp right. Lulu and I landed with a flourish at the steps that led to Snaps's domain. Otto and Charlotte caught up with us and it occurred to me that maybe leading them here might not have been a wise thing to do.

But before I could do anything, Lulu squawk-ed, "*Snaps!*" and spread her wings in a great reveal. "*SNAPS!*"

"Huh?" Otto proceeded cautiously toward the dim light up ahead.

Charlotte gripped his arm. "This is creepy!"

They peeked around the clammy stone wall into the large chamber.

"*What* is *that*?" Otto whispered.

Snaps lazed before us, snoozing next to her piles of treasure.

"That has got to be the biggest alligator I've ever seen," Charlotte gasped. "And the biggest pile of *jewels*!"

"Mystery solved," Otto murmured.

"Mystery solved," repeated Charlotte .

"Mystery solved," Lulu clucked, proud.

"Mystery solved," I cooed, contented.

Charlotte shook herself. "Let's get out of here," she whispered. "Before it wakes up. Homer, lead the way!"

CHAPTER SEVENTEEN

Of course, I knew just how to get back: I may have faltered a bit, but even underground I could sense which way was east and which was west. After a couple of turns this way and a couple that way we ended up beneath Keeler Park. A rusty, creaky iron ladder took us right back up through the open manhole near the sidewalk beneath a rain-soaked sycamore.

The summer storm was over, the rain and wind had subsided, and the raging floodwaters had become a trickling stream.

The four of us stood under the dripping tree, Lulu on Charlotte's wet shoulder and I atop Otto's soaked cap. I knew what Otto and Charlotte were thinking: "*Now what?*"

"We need to tell somebody," Charlotte offered. "We wanted to find the stolen goods...well, we did. Now we need to tell someone in charge. Real fast."

"Agreed," Otto replied. "Shouldn't we tell Grandad? And your parents?"

"Or one of those *police* officers right over there?" Charlotte pointed down the street to a couple of officers getting out of their squad car in front of Mom's Donuts. "Let's go!"

I don't know what the officers must have thought as two soggy kids raced up, one with a parrot on her shoulder and one with a pigeon on his head, but their eyebrows arched way up.

"What do we have here?" one of them asked.

"You have to follow us!" Charlotte ordered. "We know who the thief is!"

"Huh?" he asked.

"The jewel thief!" Otto added.

"The Keeler Park jewel thief!" Charlotte added.

"Underground!" Otto added.

"Underground!" Charlotte echoed.

I looked over at Lulu and cooed, "You might as well put your two cents' worth in."

"*Jewel thief! Underground!*" Lulu squawked.

Both of the police officers had expressions that could be described as a combination of amused, perplexed, and worried. One of them put his hand reassuringly on Charlotte's shoulder. "Okay, you go first, miss. Tell me slowly. What's the problem?"

Charlotte looked serious but proud to have been chosen to speak. "Well, it's really not a *problem*, it's a *solution*, you see. My name is Charlotte, and this is Otto. And thanks to Homer, there"—she pointed to me—"and Lulu here"—she gestured to her shoulder—"we have solved the notorious jewel thefts of Keeler Park. We know exactly where those jewels have gone, where to find them, and who is responsible!"

Otto hopped up and down excitedly, just like me. He couldn't wait to jump in. "And you wouldn't b*elieve* who the *thief* is!" he said. I peered over the brim of his cap. His eyes seemed as big as Mom's Donuts and his grin as wide as my wingspan.

The other officer leaned over and squinted at them both. "Okay," he said. "I'll bite. Who's the notorious thief?"

"An *alligator!*" Otto and Charlotte shouted in unison.

The officer tipped his hat back off his forehead a bit and cracked a grin. "I see," he said finally. "An alligator has stolen the jewels at Keeler Park. Uh-huh..."

"Yes!" Otto and Charlotte both said.

The police officer let out a little laugh. "Okay, you two. I mean you *four*. Joke's over. You need to go home." He glanced down at Otto's feet. His formerly white socks were squishy-wet and brown from the drain tunnel runoff. "And dry off! Where've you been?"

Otto seemed to suddenly notice how wet he was. "Oh! Well, we've been down in the sewer system," he replied, like he was talking about a Sunday stroll. "That's where we found the alligator. Snaps!"

"Snaps?"

"The giant alligator."

"Giant, *giant* alligator! Covered with jewels," Charlotte added.

"The *stolen* jewels!" Otto grinned.

The officers studied Otto's and Charlotte's faces. They must have seen they were earnest.

One of them clicked the call button on a little microphone on his belt. "Hey, Mike?" he said. "Randall here. I'm with two individuals over at Keeler Park. They say they have the scoop about the thefts. Say they know who the jewel thief is. Uh-huh. Yup. Uh-huh...yup...uh-huh. Oh, I'd say about eleven, twelve years old. Uh-huh... uh-huh...uh-huh. Yup. Roger that. Over and out."

He eyed Otto and Charlotte. "Okay...you got your wish. I have backup officers coming down to check out your story." He chuckled. "You ready to back up your story to the backup officers?"

"Yes...Sir!" Otto said.

"Call me Officer Randall. And this is Officer Jerry."

It was only a minute or two before we saw blue lights heading down Donovan Street. Two more police officers joined Officer Randall and Officer Jerry. After some further excited explaining by Otto and Charlotte and not a little convincing on their part, the four officers followed us soggy explorers back to the manhole cover.

"Homer, it's up to you, buddy," Otto said, like he was about to burst with excitement. "Find Snaps!"

Lulu looked at me and winked. "Let's do this!" she squawked. *"Snaps! Jewels! Hair clip!"*

With that, the two of us flapped our wings and spiraled down the open manhole, the humans in stumbling, rapid pursuit.

Down below, the officers pulled out their flashlights. One of them whistled. "Wowwy," she murmured, taking in the dark tunnel that stretched in front of them. "You never know where your day's gonna take you, right?"

"You said it. Look at those two birds go. We'd better hop to it!"

Lulu and I flapped and circled in place, trying to lead the humans onward, but we had to slow down and let them catch up. Now it seemed like I knew these tunnels like the back of my wing. After a myriad of now-familiar turns I soon saw the dim light of Snaps's lair.

"Here we go, Lulu!" I said. "Wait 'til the police get a load of what's up ahead!"

"They're in for a surprise!" she squawked.

Lulu and I swooped to a dramatic stop on a ledge, the humans sloshing behind us in the still-receding drainage water.

And then we all stared in awe: at the terrifyingly magnificent Snaps, stretched out before us, surrounded by a multitude of matted and tattered cats and rats.

"Holy cow! The kids weren't foolin'!" snorted one of the officers. "If I didn't see this with my own eyes, I wouldn't believe it!"

"Whoo-*eee*!" sputtered another. "How will we ever get it out of here? It'll take quite a tranquilizer to calm *that* beast."

"You got that right," Officer Jerry whispered, and gave a long, low whistle.

Finally Officer Randall spoke, dumbfounded. "Wow," he said at last. "Now *that* is an *alligator!*" He looked at Otto and at Charlotte. "Kids," he murmured, "you're one heck of an investigative team. Looks to me like the Keeler Park jewels have been found. Congratulations."

I saw Charlotte grin broadly and enfold Lulu in a hug. Otto reached up and gently took me into his hands. He smothered me with little smooches. Like I was a hero or something.

CHAPTER EIGHTEEN

The cicadas high up in the Keeler Park sycamores and elms were droning slowly, announcing the end of summer.

It had been an exciting summer for everybody. The mystery of the series of jewel thefts that had plagued Keeler Park had been solved. Thanks, mainly, to me.

"Snaps the Giant Alligator" had found a home. After living beneath the city for years, she was finally enjoying life aboveground.

And Otto and I had each found best friends.

I sat gazing with pleasure at my bulletin "board," an old plank that Otto had leaned temporarily next to my cage. Pinned to it was an accumulation of clippings gleaned from the newspaper over the past few weeks. The headlines were all in large print. Dick Tracy would have been proud.

LOCAL BOY AND
GIRL SOLVE
THEFT MYSTERY

UNDERGROUND ALLIGATOR LARGEST IN US

POLICE DEPARTMENT BESTOWS HONORS ON HOMING PIGEON, PARROT

BENEFIT AUCTION PULLS IN HUGE FUNDS FOR HOMELESS PETS

There were several photos of Otto and me, of Lulu and Charlotte, and of Snaps being hauled out of the sewer system—and apparently, that had been quite a struggle. The animal control people gave Snaps some sort of giant tranquilizer so she wouldn't chew everyone to pieces during her rescue. Then they had to find a way out of the sewer system that could accommodate her girth.

One newspaper article offered a theory as to why she was in the sewer system in the first place:

It is widely believed that the alligator was flushed down the toilet decades ago, when it was just a baby, by its uncaring owner. Apparently the giant beast, who has been named Snaps, has lived in its underground lair ever since. Thousands of dollars worth of stolen gems, silver, gold, and other valuable goods were found piled alongside the alligator. One of the officers in charge of sifting through the stolen plunder discovered a small tag and twist-tie buried in one of the piles. The tag, in child's handwriting, read:

Dear whoever finds my baby pet alligator,

Please take care of it. Dad says it's too big, but not too big to take a trip down the toilet.

Signed,
A third grader

It has taken several weeks for the newly discovered treasures to be sorted and identified. Many of the owners of the items have been located, but many have not. Items not traced to owners were given to the Animal Rescue League and auctioned off, with proceeds going to the League.

"We are still investigating how the stolen items ended up with the alligator," stated Mark Lambert from the Animal Control Board. "But one thing is clear. This is a good lesson for all would-be pet owners: only get a pet if you are willing and able to take good care of it!"

The article went on to say that Snap's American Alligator Zoo Habitat was having a ribbon-cutting ceremony. Next to the clipping Otto had pinned up an engraved invitation to the Habitat's grand opening.

I heaved a huge, contented sigh.

I heard familiar steps coming up to the loft and Otto appeared, hair slicked back. He was wearing a yellow shirt and a green-striped tie. And a big smile.

"You ready for this, Homer? Today's the big day!" Glowing, he held up another newspaper clipping.

GIANT ALLIGATOR EXHIBIT OPENS TODAY!

I cooed with excitement.

We heard feet on the wooden steps and Charlotte arrived with Lulu perched on her shoulder. Lulu had a new towel to sit on, with "LULU" embroidered on it in green and red letters to match her feathers.

"We're here!" Charlotte announced. She glanced at the bulletin board plank with the many pinned articles. "I see you've been reading the latest," she said. "'*Flushed down the toilet*'? Living down there for twenty-seven years?" She gulped. "That is so sad! Imagine her living down there all that time! Poor Snaps must've felt pretty rotten after having been flushed away. I bet she covered herself in shiny things so she'd feel better about herself. Talk about low self-esteem!"

"Yeah," Otto replied. "Exactly. And also for all those cats and rats that lived down there. Nobody cared about them, either, or ever paid any attention to them. Everybody keeps wondering how the jewels got down there...it had to have been them."

"Imagine how they felt to have someone like Snaps in charge...I bet they'd never seen anything like her!"

"And over the years she kept getting bigger and bigger, even more astonishing!"

"They treated her like a goddess!"

"They were all...outcasts." Otto said thoughtfully.

Charlotte nodded. "Maybe they felt a sense of community, and belonging. Being together."

"Well, it must feel pretty good to breathe fresh air after being underground for years," Otto said. "What a story!" He looked at me, grinning. "You ready, Homer?" He lifted me to his specially designed cap. It said "HOMER" in bright yellow letters. I happily perched on the new cap, excited about the morning ahead.

"All set! Let's go!" Charlotte replied. She started down the steps and Lulu gave a squawk of excitement.

The four of us headed through the park and then past the farmer's market and the art museum, finally reaching the city zoo. Banners were flying from each lamppost, announcing the arrival of "Snaps: Country's Amazing Gator!"

"Isn't this *the* coolest thing *ever*?" Charlotte beamed.

Otto beamed back. "I know! It's super cool."

Up ahead a man's voice boomed through a speaker: "Testing...testing...sound okay, Ed?"

"Oh my gosh, Otto," Charlotte gushed. "There's a *stage*! And a *microphone*! Are we going to have to *say* something?"

"I dunno. I'm just glad I wore a tie. People always seem smarter when they've got a tie on."

There were posters of Snaps everywhere and little carts set up selling Snaps postcards, alligator toys, mugs with alligators on them, and even snow globes with little alligators inside.

Then we saw a special cart.

"Lulu!" I gurgled. "Do you see what I see?"

Lulu squawked.

The cart was also selling postcards and toys and mugs—with pictures of Lulu and me on them! And even a Homer and Lulu snow globe! A placard next to the cart read "All Proceeds Go to the Animal Protection Fund!"

A blue-and-white-striped tent had been designated the Adoption Tent, and Snaps's past minions, all of the mangy cats and bedraggled rats, were there in cages, ready for adoption. Volunteers had vaccinated and spayed and neutered them, and they'd been bathed and brushed. They looked like they had stepped right out of a fancy pet store. A sign next to the rat cages read:

RAT!
The New Ferret!
Take One Home
TODAY!

Folding chairs were set up in front of a large blue curtain. A large crowd had gathered for the opening. Hundreds of spectators sat fanning themselves in the midmorning air, necks stretched out in hopes of catching the first glimpse of the latest zoo member, and of the boy and girl and two birds who discovered her.

At the stage a young man in a vest guided Otto and Charlotte to their seats, front and center. A tall, elegant woman lead two fluffy poodles joined them in the front row.

"Hi, Homer!" Olivia and Miss Pitty-Pat yipped. "Look! New collars! We donated our old ones to the Adoption Fund!"

I cooed back at them, my feathers proudly puffed up.

Grandad was in the front row too, of course, grinning and affectionately caressing his beloved gold watch. And there was Carlos, off to the side of the rows of chairs, strutting excitedly back and forth, waiting for the program to commence.

I glanced at the audience, looking for familiar faces. There was the lady with the orange purse, a sparkly, glittery gold bracelet back on her wrist. A man seated near the back was busily working on a newspaper crossword puzzle—*in ink!*—with his gold pen.

Finally Mayor Tomlinson stood and walked to the microphone. "Ladies, gentlemen," she began. "We are here today to commend two remarkable young people. And two remarkable birds."

The audience clapped and cheered and whistled.

The mayor continued. "Without them, we would not be celebrating a story with a happy ending. Without their unceasing investigation, attention to detail, and tireless legwork, we may never have recovered the cherished valuables that have been returned to their appreciative owners."

Another loud round of applause broke out again.

"And we may never have discovered our latest addition to the city zoo. Ladies and gentlemen, I present to you Mr. Otto Mueller and his pigeon Homer, and Miss Charlotte Perez and her parrot Lulu!"

The crowd clapped and cheered and whistled again as Otto and Charlotte stood. Otto tipped his cap and I had to flap hard to stay on, which made the crowd cheer even louder. Lulu stretched out her wings and gave as big a screech as I'd ever heard. Charlotte laughed and gave Lulu a kiss on the beak. The crowd went crazy.

With a flourish, the dark green curtain that had hidden the alligator enclosure from the audience slipped down, and everyone gasped. There sat Snaps in all her bumpy, reptilian glory, yellow-green eyes glinting in the sun. I heard hundreds of little clicks across the lawn as people took pictures. A spontaneous explosion of applause filled the air.

Snaps lay basking next to a newly created shallow pond, luxuriating on a warm, muddy strip of shoreline. Instead of jewels and shiny trinkets, she lay nestled among clusters of cattails that lined the pond, the surface of which was dotted with fragrant white water lilies. The sunshine and summertime breeze were caressing and sweet-smelling, vastly different from the stagnant air and dark recesses of the sewage tunnel.

As she lounged there, grinning at the photographers and the admiring onlookers, I saw her spy Lulu and me smiling from the stage. She waved a giant, clawed paw, her eyes moist. "Thanks, guys," she croaked.

What a summer!

It had been a challenge...a stolen treasured watch,

a drainage tunnel during a deluge, a giant alligator! But overcoming a challenge came with quite a reward: with my new best friend I had made others happy.

What better reward is there?